CHANGING TIDES

LOBSTER BAY 2

MEREDITH SUMMERS

Pull up a beach chair and dig your toes in the sand as life continues in Lobster Bay.

Things are changing for Jane Miller. Just as her friend Claire gets on her feet again from a near catastrophe with her bakery, Jane faces challenges with the beachfront bed-and-breakfast her family has owned for generations. Her mother is no longer able to run things, and Jane finds herself in charge.

It's a big change, especially since Jane expected to be retired by now, but she's promised her mother she will carry on the family legacy. Too bad she doesn't know very much about running an inn.

But luck is on her side when she comes across a new furry friend, Cooper, who helps her navigate the challenge. It doesn't hurt that Cooper's new owner is easy on the eyes—even though Jane vowed she'd never look again.

Naturally she also has Claire and Maxi to lean on.

Claire is happy with her new bakery and new beau, but Maxi is facing some changes of her own. Will Maxi find the strength to finally pursue her passion for art even while her marriage may be in trouble?

Visit Lobster Bay on the coast of Maine today, and find out how these three friends navigate the changes in their lives.

This book can be read as a stand-alone story, but it will be a lot more fun if you read book 1 first, as you will get more background details about some of the characters in this story.

CHAPTER 1

*J*ane Miller stood in the doorway of the private room at the Tall Pines Memory Care Facility and watched her mother, Addie. She was sitting in her old rocking chair beside the window, a pencil in her hand and her gaze intent on a word-search book that was laid out in her lap. The look of contentment on her mother's face brought Jane a mixture of relief and anxiety. Relief because her mother was happy. Anxiety because she didn't know how she was going to continue paying the bill.

The monthly cost was much more than their failing family inn, Tides, was bringing in. Jane didn't have any savings or much for retirement, so hopefully she could get some aid for her mother. That was actually one of the reasons for her visit. She had an appointment with the financial director in a few minutes but wanted to pop in and see her mother first.

She pushed the door open, and Addie looked over and smiled. It was no wonder her mother felt at home here. Jane had had one of her best friends, Maxi Stevens, help decorate the room, and it held all of her mother's familiar things from her room at Tides. The blue-and-white wedding-ring quilt that Jane's grandmother had stitched by hand, the bird figurines that Dad would give to Mom every wedding anniversary, the family photos, including Jane's favorite of her and her sister, Andie, arm in arm at the beach.

Maxi had brought in a few new things that she'd artfully placed here and there, too, and the overall effect was stunning. Jane wasn't surprised—as an artist, Maxi was bursting with creativity.

Jane perched on the edge of the bed. "How are you feeling today, Mom?"

"Wonderful." Addie's smile turned to a frown. "Shouldn't you be downstairs feeding the guests?"

Apparently, Maxi had done such a good job of emulating Addie's room, down to the small television in the corner, that Addie thought she was still at Tides. But since she seemed so content, Jane didn't want to enlighten her. Let her think what she wanted as long as it made her happy. "Brenda can handle the guests this morning."

Brenda had worked for Tides as their chief cook and general helper for decades. At first, she'd worked under Addie's instruction and later had helped fill in where Addie's memory lapses left off. When it became too much, Jane had retired from her job as an accountant in order to help Brenda and take over running the inn. She'd always hoped to keep her mom at the inn, but that wasn't meant to be. Luckily Brenda knew as much as Jane did about running the place, and she could comfortably leave her in charge.

"Brenda is a good cook, but she isn't the face of Tides. You should be down there making sure that their stay is a pleasant one. The guests won't come back if it isn't."

Apparently, Addie hadn't noticed that Tides had only had one guest for most of the summer. That was probably for the best too.

A change of subject was in order. "I brought you a chocolate chip muffin." Jane held up a white bakery bag.

Addie put down the pen and reached for the bag, peering in with a delighted smile. "These are my favorite!"

"Claire made them." Jane wondered if her mother

would remember Claire Turner, her lifelong friend and owner of Sandcastles Bakery in Lobster Bay.

"She makes the best muffins," Addie said around a bite. She seemed to remember who Claire was today.

"She does," Jane agreed.

Addie glanced over Jane's shoulder into what was sure to be an unfamiliar hallway. Jane expected her to become confused or upset. Instead, her mother set aside the far-from-finished word search and pen and asked, "Where is Andrea?"

Good question. Jane's older sister had once been her idol, back when Jane was a freshman in high school and Andie a senior. But when Andie left town for college and never looked back, Jane realized that she hadn't meant that much to her sister. None of them had, if the infrequency of her visits was any indication. Sure, she'd come back when Jane's baby—and then her husband—had died. She'd been there when their dad had gotten sick. But she never stayed long. Why would it be any different now?

Of course, her absence might be because Jane hadn't told Andie the full truth. Not that she'd wanted to leave Andie out of the decision-making process, but everything had happened so fast. Tall Pines was the best facility around, and they didn't often have openings. Jane had jumped at the chance, and there hadn't been time to wait for her sister to fly out to mull over the decision. Besides, Andie hadn't been here this past year watching their mother decline. Jane had done all the heavy lifting and felt she was best positioned to make the decision.

Still, she did have a tiny seed of guilt that she could have tried harder to let Andie know what was really going on. Hadn't she glossed over the real state of affairs in her texts and phone calls? And maybe she had felt responsible that their mother had wandered off and didn't want her big sister to think she'd fallen down on the job of making sure their mother was safe.

Andrea knew about the change in their mother's living situation. Jane hadn't gone into details, certainly not over a voicemail message, but she'd left enough information for Andie to get in touch. So far, they hadn't been able to connect. It probably didn't make much difference, though. She doubted Andie would want to come out and help. She'd probably be relieved that Jane was taking care of everything and happy to stay back in New York City, where she worked for Christie's as an antiques appraiser.

"Andie is at work right now." Jane didn't want to disappoint her mother and tell her that her oldest daughter most likely wouldn't be coming.

Addie latched onto Jane's arm. Her expression had

lost its dreamy cast and was fully serious. The lines around her mouth and nose were deeper than ever. "You'll convince her to visit, won't you, Jane? She listens to you."

No, she doesn't.

Jane bit her lip. She didn't want to make a promise she couldn't keep. "I'll try. Speaking of which, I'd better get going."

"That's right. You make sure breakfast is coming along. I don't want Brenda to scare them all away with her crankiness. You know how she gets while she's cooking."

Brenda was perhaps the sweetest soul in Lobster Bay. A bit surly if someone got in her way while she was cooking, but she would never be cranky to a guest.

Nevertheless, Jane promised. "I will."

"Good. But before you go, you better find my sweater."

"Sweater?" Jane glanced into the closet. She'd moved all of her mother's clothes over but hadn't finished writing her name on the tags yet as recommended by the staff here. "Which one?"

"The sea-green one with the buttons shaped like seashells down the front. I can't find it anywhere."

Leave it to Addie to forget where she was but remember the exact description of her favorite sweater.

"I'll help you find it," Jane assured her. She tried to keep the frown off her face and out of her voice as she stood and turned toward the dresser. Unfortunately, despite searching through the dresser and the closet under Addie's supervision, she didn't find the sweater. "I'm sorry, Mom, it's not here."

"I knew it!"

"Knew what?"

"Sadie Thompson took it. She's always borrowing my clothes and not giving them back!"

Sadie Thompson had been her mother's best friend in high school. Apparently, they'd had some sort of falling out back then and hadn't spoken in years. When her mother's memory had first started to slip, she'd mentioned Sadie a few times. It was funny how the mind worked.

"I don't think it was Sadie. Let me have a look through Tides and see if I can find the sweater for you."

Addie beamed. "Thank you. I have to wear it tonight for my big date with that nice Bradford fellow!"

Jane smiled. Addie had a crush on the owner of the new bread bakery in town, Rob Bradford. Rob had been very sweet to Addie and had actually been the one who had told Jane about Tall Pines. No point in telling Addie that Rob was young enough to be her son and that he'd fallen pretty hard for Jane's friend Claire.

Since her mother thought she was still a teenager some-times, she'd let her mother believe what she wanted to believe about Rob.

Jane kissed her on the cheek. "We'll get it to you in time. I have to go now. Goodbye, Mom."

Jane hurried out of the room. She didn't want to be late for her meeting with Wendy Martinelli, the finance director for Tall Pines. Having her mother's future at Tall Pines secured financially would be a huge relief.

Wendy Martinelli was in her forties, with only a hint of crinkles around her eyes betraying her age. She had round cheeks, a ready smile, and straight white teeth. Jane liked her immediately.

"Hi, I'm Jane Miller. We spoke on the phone. Am I late?"

"Right on time." Wendy indicated for her to sit, and Jane folded herself into the chair opposite her desk.

Wendy clicked a couple of keys on her computer and opened a manila folder in front of her. "You're here to inquire about Medicaid for your mother, Adelaide?"

"Yes. I signed the release forms for you to check into her credit history and dropped off the completed form last weekend when we moved her in."

The woman nodded, a strand of blond hair falling across her cheek. "Yes, I see that here." Her smile dimmed as she closed the file and set it lightly atop her keyboard. "Unfortunately, we have a problem."

"What sort of problem? Did I forget to sign something?"

Wendy's eyes softened as she met Jane's gaze. "I'm afraid your mother doesn't qualify for Medicaid."

How was that possible? Jane had discovered that Addie had spent what little retirement savings she'd had over the past few years, and with bookings almost nonexistent at the inn, she had no income. "You must have made a mistake. It's there in the financials. She doesn't have much in the way of retirement savings. Every penny has gone into the upkeep of our family inn, Tides."

"That's the problem. Tides is a premium beachfront property. That's too large an asset to qualify for Medicaid. If you sold the inn, we might be able to discuss this again, but you'd probably have too much money to qualify then." Wendy looked at her with sympathy. "Unless your mother had signed the property over to another family member at least six years ago."

Jane shook her head. As far as she knew, the property was still in her parents' name. "So my only option is to sell it?"

Sell the inn? For a split second, she considered it. No more dealing with guests. No more worrying about food deliveries and room cleaning. Jane would have *free time* again. But she'd promised her mother she would never sell. It was their family legacy.

"If you sell, then you could use the proceeds to pay for your mother's care. Once that money runs out, then maybe we could revisit the option of Medicare."

"Maybe? What if the money runs out and she gets denied?"

"I'm afraid that's a possibility. The money would last for a while, but we have no idea what the laws and rules will be in a few years. You might have to care for her at home."

Jane almost laughed. She'd lost money on the sale of her modest home so she could move in to Tides to care for her mother and help her run the inn. If they sold Tides, there wouldn't be any home in which to care for Addie, never mind any money to pay for the care she now needed.

Jane took a deep breath. She'd have to figure something out. "Okay, thanks for your time."

They shook hands, and Jane left the office.

Her mind whirling with options, she barely noticed where she was going as she walked down the hallway, out the front door, and along the sidewalk next to the manicured landscaping that led to the parking lot.

Bookings were down at Tides and the inn needed repairs, but it had once turned a tidy profit. Maybe she could do some advertising or have some sort of sale like her friend Claire had done for her bakery. If she could fill the inn with guests and maybe find some additional income, she'd be able to pay for Addie's room at Tall Pines and—

Oof!

Jane squeaked as she toppled backward into a fat, leafy bush. A big golden ball of fur leaped after her, a wet nose touched her chin, and she found herself staring into a pair of deep-brown eyes that shone with an eagerness to make friends. A leash dangled from the dog's collar, and Jane grabbed it so the golden retriever wouldn't take off.

"Cooper!" called a man. "Cooper, come back here!"

Jane scrambled out of the bush. Cooper seemed happy to stay by her side, staring up at her with soulful brown eyes. His happy demeanor made her smile.

"I'm so sorry." The man expertly hooked his fingers into the red collar around the dog's throat and tugged him back.

"It's no problem." Jane handed him the end of the

leash then brushed herself off and picked a leaf out of her hair.

Cooper strained at the hold on his collar, trying desperately to reach her again. Jane crouched and rubbed Cooper's neck, dodging his wet kisses.

"Cooper, stop that!" The man, tall and in his late thirties or maybe early forties, flashed her a chagrined smile. "I'm sorry. He's usually much better behaved than this or I wouldn't bring him."

Jane looked up at the man. "Is he yours?"

He shook his head, and his smile widened. He had a very nice smile, probably the most noticeable thing about him aside from his height and curly brown hair. "He belongs to my grandpa. I'm Mike Henderson."

He stuck his hand out, and Jane stood and shook it. "Jane Miller. Is your grandfather here at Tall Pines?"

Mike nodded. "He's one of the oldest residents. Lived on his own in Lobster Bay until he hit ninety-five. Now he needs more help."

"Oh." Jane blinked, mulling over the name in her head. It was slightly familiar. "I run the bed-and-break-fast in Lobster Bay."

"Small world," Mike said with a grin. Cooper had retreated to Mike's side, who reached down and gave the canine a pat. Cooper wagged his tail at Jane as if to suggest that it wouldn't be a bad idea for her to pet him too.

"I just moved my mother into this facility. Has your grandfather been here long? How do you like it?"

"He hasn't been here long. The transition has been tough. That's why I'm staying in town for a while, to get him settled and make sure he gets to see Cooper. Cooper's visits really help."

"You don't live near here?"

"No. Seattle," Mike said. "We don't have family any closer to help Gramps, and I can telecommute. How does your mother like it so far?"

"She seems to be adjusting well."

"Good. It's a nice place." Mike glanced at Tall Pines. "Well, I suppose I better get in there. Nice meeting you."

Jane watched them walk to the door. Cooper looked back at her as if to say, "See you later." Jane hoped he would. Something about the golden retriever made her problems seem a little smaller.

She walked to her car, her spirits revived. She was on her way to meet her two best friends for morning coffee, and that always picked up her mood. She was sure they'd be able to help her figure out what to do about the fees at Tall Pines.

Things were looking up... until her phone chimed

with a text from her sister. She'd left Andie a message about their mother a few days ago, and they'd been playing phone and text tag ever since. Jane wanted to talk to her in person. She owed her that, and the information was too much to pass back and forth in messages.

She threw the phone onto the car seat. It had taken Andie long enough to respond, and she could wait a few more hours. Jane had to stop at Tides to take care of a few things before meeting her friends for coffee, and she didn't want to be late. They had a lot to talk about.

CHAPTER 2

*A*ndie Miller glanced down at the phone on her desk. Jane hadn't returned her text yet. The lack of communication had her worried. Jane's last message about their mother had had a ring of foreboding to it. There was something she wasn't telling Andie. Should Andie go home? But why? Jane would handle everything, and that was the way her sister wanted things, wasn't it? It sure seemed that way since Jane never asked for her opinion or her help.

But was that really the way Jane wanted things, or was it because Andie had practically abandoned them by taking off right after high school and only going back when something bad happened? Like when Jane's infant son had died... and then her husband. And when their father had gotten sick. Even on those horrible occasions, Andie had provided comfort as best she could and then taken off back to her career as soon as possible.

It wasn't that Andie didn't like her family—she loved them dearly. But there just wasn't much for her back in Lobster Bay. Her career as an antiques appraiser necessitated that she live in a city where antiques collectors and auction houses were prevalent, not in a small seaside beach town. Besides, the last time she'd gone home, her mom had been doing fairly well. A little more forgetful, but she was able to manage, and Jane was helping out at the inn.

Andie loved her job. She'd always been enthralled with the past, and as an antiques collector, restorer, and appraiser, she had the privilege of handling unique pieces of history that were hundreds of years old. She was good at her job too. Her expertise and passion were what had granted her a senior position at Christie's. Her drive and her willingness to put in long hours had been what had made her boss, Doug, look at her in an entirely different light.

Her *married* boss. Surely she wasn't out of line for pushing him to get that divorce he had claimed for months he was on the cusp of delivering to his wife? They were estranged. They were unhappy. Doug had been happy with Andie these past seven months.

Or so he said. Yet ever since she'd brought the divorce up a week ago, Doug had found more and more reasons not to be in the office. And now he wasn't even returning her texts.

Andie looked away from the phone and concentrated on the ivory-inlaid box she'd been inspecting. Everything would work out fine. Doug was probably just busy. The box, with its intricate design and sterling silver interior, was in perfect condition. She noted so in her documentation before glancing at her phone again. Nothing from Doug or Jane.

"Andrea, how would you catalogue this?"

Susie Thornburg, the fresh-out-of-college new hire was looking at her expectantly with her wide brown eyes. Andie supposed that Susie was a good kid, and she did seem to have a love for antiques and a good work ethic. But Andie wasn't the most patient person, and being tasked with training an overly eager apprentice almost thirty years her junior really wasn't her cup of tea.

She looked at the item in question and very slowly, very patiently pointed out, "I just catalogued that. It's under metalware. See here?" She pointed to the entry in the computer, a few lines above in the Recent Entries column.

Susie laughed brightly. "Oh. I guess I'm still on vacation time."

They each returned to their work, but the silence didn't last long. It was just as well. If Andie didn't find some distraction, she was going to set the world record for most number of times a woman has checked her phone for messages and found none.

Susie asked in a chipper tone, "So, what's up with Doug? Shouldn't he have checked on us by now? He usually does."

Susie didn't know about Andie's affair with their boss. No one did. At first, Andie had accepted Doug's reasoning for keeping their affair secret. After all, it had started so fast, crossing the line from innocent to a deeper connection almost before she knew what was happening.

Neither of them wanted it to be a problem at work. Even though the company didn't have any rules against people dating, Doug had recently been separated from his wife, and it was awkward. Andie didn't want her coworkers to think she was getting the good jobs because of her relationship with Doug, even though everyone knew she'd earned those jobs with years of dedication and hard work and had been awarded them before the relationship started.

But as time went on, she should have picked up on

the fact that Doug never really wanted to go to any parties or out in public. He didn't introduce her to any of his friends. She should have realized that meant that he wasn't as *separated* from his wife as he'd led her to believe.

She steered Susie to safer waters. "Who knows? So, how was your trip down to Florida to see your mom?"

If nothing else, Susie was always happy to chatter about her own life. Andie didn't mind so much. The girl's enthusiasm was contagious, and she had a nice manner about her. Maybe if Andie was younger, they might have been friends that went out for drinks together after work. Maybe they would now, even though Andie was probably Susie's mother's age.

As Susie talked about her visit home, Andie felt a weird pang of homesickness. She didn't often miss her hometown, and even though she never cared to visit there, it had a lot of things going for it. The sugar-sand beaches, the smell of the ocean. The fresh lobster. But it was a small town, and Andie had always wanted more. That was one reason why she'd left and never looked back—and why she'd treated the boy she'd been head over heels for so terribly. She'd been scared she'd be stuck in Lobster Bay waiting for him to come home from the navy. Or never come home at all. But that had been decades ago now, and it was all water under the bridge.

Stifling a sigh, Andie finished cataloguing the box and moved on to the next piece, a jade figurine of an elephant with a raised trunk. She put on her bifocals to inspect it more closely. Not everything in this room was rare or old. The appraisers sometimes bid on estate sales and had to wade through them to find the chunks of gold hidden amid the manure. But whenever she did discover a rare find, it always gave Andie a little thrill.

When she'd left for college, she'd wanted to be an archaeologist. But experience had soon taught her that she was not the outdoorsy type. Nevertheless, history fascinated her, and she always dreamed of making that one big discovery. A document from the founding of the country hidden behind a painting, a long-lost diary, an important piece of jewelry lost by a queen whose government had been overthrown. Maybe it was a fantasy to hope for something so big, but it was a buzz that had gotten inside Andie's stomach and never left. It filled her with breathless anticipation every time she picked up a new piece.

But this figurine wasn't it. By her estimate, given its style and the wear of the grooves carved into it, it was from the early 1900s. She needed to consult her reference book to be sure.

As she moved toward the book, Susie's chipper voice washed over her again, piercing her sense of calm.

"No fair."

Andie frowned, looking up. She pulled her bifocals off her nose and perched them on top of her head again. "What isn't fair?"

"The way Doug is playing favorites."

Andie drew herself up. Was she referring to Andie? She couldn't possibly know about their affair.

Susie continued, "She's been here for less time than me!"

Andie turned to face her associate head-on. "Pardon me?"

"Elise," Susie answered with a dismissive wave of her hand. "I have a funny feeling about her, with her bright smile and chirpy attitude and supermodel figure. She might be getting special treatment. She just got a big appraisal job."

"She's getting prime jobs? Already?" Andie wondered if Susie was exaggerating. "That can't be right. I'm due to fly out for the next one."

Andie couldn't be losing her prestige to a new appraiser. She had clawed her way up to get to where she was. She worked long hours, even weekends. In the back of her mind, she had always feared that as soon as she passed fifty, she would start to get overlooked despite her expertise. But it hadn't happened. And now...

Susie patted Andie's arm. "Don't worry about it. I'm sure she'll choke and get pulled off the next run. I mean, sure, she has a good eye for antiques, but it's nothing compared to yours."

"Which job did she get?" Maybe it was a job that would conflict with a bigger job they intended to give to Andie?

Susie shrugged. "Vanderburgh in Palm Springs. It looks like a good one. I'm sure she'll be calling you any minute now for advice."

Andie pressed her lips together. It *was* a good one. Was that why Doug had ignored her texts? Andie was busy with this job, but they could have handed the grunt work off to Elise with Susie to assist and flown Andie to Palm Springs. Why would they let Elise go on her own? The last few jobs, she'd had to call Andie for advice on almost every item.

Andie sat back at her desk and glanced at her phone. Still no texts. Maybe a visit to Lobster Bay wouldn't be such a bad idea. She *was* worried about her mother. She hadn't seen her in almost a year. They'd talked on the phone, but sometimes her mother had been confused. And there was nothing like seeing someone face-to-face.

Maybe if Doug saw that she wasn't sitting around here waiting for him to call, he might realize what he was missing. Then again, a little voice inside her cautioned that maybe she didn't want him to realize that. Not for personal reasons, but she still wanted to be his choice for the good jobs. If she left, would Elise replace her as the new favorite?

That was ridiculous. A respectable auction house like Christie's wouldn't replace an experienced veteran like Andie with a newcomer like Elise. She checked the schedule of upcoming appraisals on her computer.

There was a big estate that was expected to go on the market soon. Robert Richhaven had a collection that antiques collectors would weep over. No one had seen it in recent years, given his failing health and his propensity to return to his reclusive ways at the slightest provocation. However, with no children and distant relatives more interested in selling the estate fast, this could be Andie's find of a lifetime. More than anything, she was determined to be sent to the Richhaven Estate when it went up for auction. But that wouldn't happen for a few weeks.

She had time to go back home and let Doug see just how important she was for this operation. Without her here, Elise would have to sink or swim on her own. Andie didn't want her to sink. She didn't wish her, or Christie's, any harm, but if the higher-ups thought she was ready to go out on jobs on her own, then she guessed it was only fair that they saw how she could handle things without Andie helping in the background. Besides, Andie had a lot of vacation time accrued and had to use it by the end of the year.

She picked up her phone and started shopping for a plane ticket to Maine.

CHAPTER 3

*B*y the time Jane drove up the pebbled drive in front of Tides, she'd come to terms with the fact that paying for Addie's care might not be as easy as she'd hoped.

The silence of the inn was another reminder that moving her mother to Tall Pines was the right thing to do. Bookings had been down drastically this year, and Jane had been too busy trying to make sure her mother didn't wander off or leave the stove burner on to even think about how to rectify that. Now she didn't have much of a choice, not if she was going to keep her promise to her mother. She was going to have to figure out a way to bring in more business.

Jane was good at finances, though. She could juggle

bills in her sleep. She could find a way to make this work.

Her footsteps echoed on the smooth, worn floors of the old Victorian house. Although the house was in working order, it had retained its rustic air as well as a constant list of minor repairs that needed to be handled. Jane liked its charm. In a way, she was glad that in appearance the inn hadn't changed much since she'd been a child. There was a nostalgia that hung from the eaves and gables, a cozy feeling of safety. If running the inn didn't go hand in hand with interacting with so many strangers, Jane might enjoy it a lot more. Of course, lately there hadn't even been that many strangers—just old Mrs. Weatherlee, who had been here for two weeks. She was quiet and mostly kept to herself, so at least Jane didn't have to pretend to be an extrovert around her.

Jane proceeded to the kitchen, where Brenda was washing out a thick yellowware mixing bowl.

Brenda was a cheerful woman with a round face and a bright smile. She liked to hum while she cleaned the kitchen, but she was always off tune. Jane cleared her throat to announce her arrival.

Brenda straightened with a jump. "Jane! You're back." She recovered from her shock quickly, still holding the dripping bowl. "How did the meeting at Tall Pines go?"

"Not as expected," Jane admitted with a grimace. "I'm just about to head into town to meet with Claire and Maxi, but I wanted to check in and make sure you didn't need anything."

Brenda's face creased with concern. The sixty-five-year-old woman was more like family than hired help. She'd been a close sidekick for Addie after Jane's father had died and had taken care of her as her dementia progressed over the past several years. Brenda was as concerned about Addie getting good care as Jane was.

"Don't worry," Jane assured her. "Medicaid won't pay for Mom, but everything will be okay."

"How can I help?" Brenda asked.

Jane sighed, running her finger along the well-worn surface of the rectangular pine kitchen table. The table had been there since before Jane had been born. Maybe even since before her mother had been born. She remembered many family meals at this table. She couldn't let that all slip away now. "I guess just keep cooking your awesome breakfasts. I'm going to have to figure out how to get more guests to the inn, and your food is the key."

"Oh, I don't know about that." Brenda waved off

the compliment, but Jane could see that she was pleased.

Jane kissed her cheek. "Speaking of that, I guess I better play innkeeper and go make sure Mrs. Weatherlee is enjoying her breakfast."

"Stop and have some yourself," Brenda encouraged her. She turned her back to continue loading the dishwasher. "There's plenty there, and it will only go to waste if somebody doesn't eat it."

"Claire always keeps a muffin ready for me when we meet in the mornings."

Brenda *tsk*ed. "You need to eat more than a muffin. It's no wonder you're so skinny."

Some people would say those words with praise. With Brenda, who wore the evidence of her good cooking with a comfort that Jane could never emulate, it was a chastisement.

"If there's still some left over, I'll eat it for lunch or supper."

That was a common theme in Jane's life. The inn served one full breakfast, and Brenda usually went all-in with her meals. Even though they only had one guest, Jane wouldn't be surprised to see piles of eggs, bacon, and toast laid out neatly along with the basket of muffins she made sure to keep stocked in from Claire's bakery and the fresh-baked bread from Bradford

Breads. It wasn't unusual for Jane to have breakfast food for supper, just so it wouldn't go to waste. Brenda had pared the volume of her cooking down considerably, but she hadn't gotten the hang of cooking for the smaller amount of guests yet.

Through the swinging kitchen door was the dining room. Whereas the kitchen was an eclectic mix of modern and rustic—including a walk-in refrigerator, which was well used during the busy season—the dining room was all seaside elegance.

There were several tables set up so that guests could have their own private dining experiences. The tables were covered in pristine white linen. The mahogany-backed chairs all matched, their talon-and-ball feet resting on the jewel-toned Oriental rug that covered most of the wide pine flooring.

The ceilings were ten feet tall, and a row of floor-to-ceiling French doors faced the ocean, providing an astounding view of golden sand and cobalt waves. The windows were flanked by cobalt-blue silk drapes that had been custom made in Jane's grandmother's day. The doors were cracked open, and the edges of the drapes fluttered in the breeze.

One tiny white-haired old lady sat at a table next to the window, slowly cutting into the Belgian waffle on her plate. Brenda had certainly outdone herself with the meal today, with a bowl of fresh fruit on the table next to the muffins and a staggering stack of waffles. Jane would be eating them for days since Mrs. Weatherlee was barely five feet tall, and Jane would be surprised if she finished even one waffle.

"Good morning, Mrs. Weatherlee. How are you today?"

The woman turned from the window, smiling. "Wonderful. Who wouldn't be with a plate full of food and this gorgeous view?" She patted her lips with her napkin.

Jane glanced out the window. The woman had a point. "I hope breakfast is satisfactory."

"Of course. You always have the best breakfasts here. How is your mother, dear?"

For an old lady, Mrs. Weatherlee was sharp as a tack and didn't miss a thing. She'd been here for over two weeks and had witnessed some of Addie's less lucid moments. She knew that Addie was now residing at Tall Pines. "She's doing great. Thanks for asking."

Mrs. Weatherlee nodded slowly, her cornflower-blue eyes sympathetic. "It's hard, but you made the right decision. Now you can focus on building this inn back to what it once was. You are going to do that, aren't you?"

Jane glanced around at the empty tables. Could she? "I'm going to try."

Mrs. Weatherlee nodded. "Good, then. Don't worry. Everything will be all right." She tucked back into her waffle.

Mrs. Weatherlee's positive attitude gave Jane new confidence, and she started back toward the front. She'd better get a move on if she wanted to meet her two best friends, Claire and Maxi, at Claire's bakery, Sandcastles.

She stepped out onto the front porch in time to see a blond woman step out of her bubblegum-pink Mini Cooper, carrying a sheaf of papers in her arms.

Oh no! What was *she* doing here?

Sandee Harris was a local realtor, and yes, Jane had reached out to a realty company to get an estimate on Tides, but she'd been dealing with Dorian Wells, *not* Sandee. Not only was Sandee mean, condescending, and generally annoying, she was also the woman Claire's husband had cheated on Claire with. Claire was one of Jane's best friends, and she'd rather deal with a pit of vipers than give any business to Sandee Harris.

"Janey! Oh, good. Looks like I've just caught you!"

Janey? Where had that come from? "Just Jane, actually. What are you doing here? I was dealing with Dorian."

As Sandee rounded her car, she pressed the key fob in her hand. The car chirped as the doors locked. As if she needed to lock it here in Lobster Bay where the crime rate was practically zero. Just showed how out of touch she was.

"Dorian's under the weather, so she asked me to fill you in." Sandee smiled as if oblivious to the fact that Jane didn't want her here.

A lock of hair falling into her face, Sandee—just barely forty, another blow to Claire's fifty-year-old ego —flipped through the folder in her hand with finger-nails painted the same color as her car. She held her lower lip between her teeth as she fished out a page and set it on the top. Then she offered the entire folder to Jane.

"Here's the appraisal. If you'd like to list the property as is, I think we should start at the first number I've listed on that sheet and take no less than $50,000 under the list price."

The list price was appallingly low. Jane stared at the paper. Her ears rang with the numbers. Numbers that didn't look right.

And Jane knew her numbers.

"You want to list the property for *this?*"

Not even the tiniest flicker of doubt passed over the agent's face. "As is, yes."

"We're an oceanfront property! And it's a viable business too. It's worth at least twice that!"

Sandee scrunched her nose. "Is it? You need new siding or at the very least a new coat of paint. You're on town water, but the pipes are old and will need to be replaced inside the next five years. Same with the furnace, the hot-water tank, the windows... do I really have to keep going? And tell me, Janey, how many customers do you have renting rooms right now?"

Jane pursed her lips and refused to open them. She had only one. And Sandee did have a point about the condition. But still, she had been hoping that the property itself would be worth more, just in case she needed to sell. Even if it needed a few minor things done, it *was* an investment property.

"We're the only bed-and-breakfast in Lobster Bay," Jane protested. She couldn't believe that her childhood home and inheritance was worth so little.

Sandee looked pitying. "But there are plenty of homes rented through Airbnb now, and nice inns in the neighboring towns. And if Tides isn't full right now at peak season, then I doubt your balance sheet is favorable. You have to look at this realistically, Janey, because that's what a buyer will do."

The page crinkled as Jane stuffed it into the folder and snapped it shut. "Well, Tides isn't for sale."

Sandee took the folder. "No? But you asked for the appraisal."

"I changed my mind. I'm not selling, especially not for that price." She couldn't afford to. That would only pay for a few years of Addie's care, and what would she do after that? Never mind the question of what she, herself, would live on. She'd lost money on the sale of her own house when she'd had to let it go to live here, and her retirement savings were pitiful.

"Oh, well let me know if you change your mind." Sandee grabbed the folder and made off toward her car.

Jane blew out a breath as she watched the blonde fold herself back inside the small car.

"You okay?" The voice came from the corner of the porch up near the ceiling, and Jane looked up to see Sally Littlefield standing atop the second-to-last rung of a ladder with a caulking gun in her hand as she fixed the sealant on a window. Sally, the town handywoman, was in her seventies but still spry in both body and mind. Her expression grim, the woman set down the caulking gun on the top of the ladder and quickly descended to the bottom. She wiped her hands on her overalls as she turned to Jane.

"I'm fine," Jane said, not wanting to burden Sally with her problems.

"I heard what Sandee said to you. You really aren't thinking about selling, are you?"

"Not really. But it's expensive to have Mom in Tall Pines, and I just wanted a number in case things don't pick up here at the inn."

"I don't know what number that wicked woman put in that file you're holding, and it's none of my business, but if I were you, I wouldn't trust her."

"No?"

Sally shook her head. "She isn't good people. My guess is she's up to something sketchy."

"That doesn't make sense. She's a real estate agent. She makes a commission. She *wants* me to sell for the highest price because then she'll get a bigger payout."

Sally narrowed her eyes. She shoved her hands in her pockets and rocked back on her heels. "Ah-yuh, if you say so."

"You don't sound convinced."

"I'm not. That woman always has something up her sleeve. Besides," Sally added as she swept her arm toward the whitewashed Victorian house, "you can't sell. Tides has been a pillar of this town for decades. You used to be booked well in advance for all three good-weather months and some guests in the winter too. I wouldn't give up on it just yet."

Jane didn't want to. For one, it looked like selling

wasn't going to gain her much anyway, and for two, she'd promised her mother. But how in the world was she going to get business to pick up? This wasn't her area of expertise.

Sally added, "And if you ask me, the repairs aren't so extensive. Ah-yuh, you might have to replace those pipes or furnace eventually, but they're still in good working order. It's the weatherproofing that I think is the most important, and there's a lot of little cosmetic things. But I have to tell you, I'm not sure I can handle it all myself."

Jane had a sinking feeling. "You can't? It's too complicated?" The work of finding a trusted contractor and negotiating a price and payment plan she could afford was another straw on her back. One she didn't need added right now.

"I can do it, but it would take me a while. Maybe months."

It was still summer. Surely, she would be able to finish before the snow set in.

Sally patted Jane's hand with a smile. "But you're in luck. I happen to know that Shane Flannery is back in town."

Jane opened her mouth then shut it again. "Shane Flannery?" A face flashed in front of her mind's eye, dulled by the years since high school. Surely it couldn't be the same...

"Retired from the navy," Sally confirmed. "And he's looking for carpentry work in the area. I've seen his work, and he's very good. Inexpensive, too, since he's just setting up his business." She winked. "Plus, he's not too sore on the eyes, if you understand me."

Jane smiled weakly. "I bet he isn't." The Shane Flannery she had known, back when her sister had dated him in high school, had been the athletic type. Filled with energy and smiles, radiating a magnetic sort of charm, and so head over heels for Andrea that it had been adorable. Jane seemed to recall that he'd wanted to get married, but Andie had gone off to greener pastures. Broke the guy's heart, from what she remembered.

"I'll look him up," she promised Sally.

And she meant it too. Obviously Shane and her sister had a history, but that had been decades ago, and Andie wasn't here. Jane needed help from somewhere, and she couldn't afford to be picky.

"Good." Sally turned back to the ladder. She paused with her hand on the rung and looked over her shoulder, her white braid obscuring half her face. "Don't you give up on this place, Jane," she said fiercely. "It's your family legacy. Family is everything."

Jane knew that. Family was everything to her too.

The problem was she didn't have much family left. Her husband and son had passed on from this world. Her mother was fading away. Her sister didn't return her calls. All she had was this ramshackle inn and the memories it contained. But those memories still warmed her at night, and that was something.

She couldn't give it up, wouldn't give it up, without a fight. Somehow she had to bring more business to Tides. Then maybe she'd be able to scrape together enough money to pay for Addie's care and eke out a modest living for herself. One thing was for sure, she had to make the effort or she wouldn't be able to live with herself.

But even though she didn't have much in the way of family, she wasn't in this all alone. She had the two best friends in the world waiting for her, and between the three of them she was sure they'd figure something out.

CHAPTER 4

*C*laire Turner took a sip of her dark roast coffee as she watched Maxi whip up a quick sketch of the front of Claire's bakery and cafe on the white napkin she'd plucked from the center of the table. They were seated at one of the round tables nestled on the sidewalk outside. The sun was shining, and Claire could almost hear the ocean waves crashing on the beach at the end of the road.

"Jane *is* coming, isn't she?" Maxi split her attention between the napkin and the front of the bakery before ducking her head again to add a potted plant near the door.

"I think so. She texted me earlier and told me she had to visit with Addie first." Claire looked down the street to see if she could spot Jane. She usually walked up from Tides, as it was only a few blocks away. "You don't think something's wrong with Addie, do you?"

Maxi glanced up. "I hope not." The breeze tugged at the strands of silvery blond hair that had slid over Maxi's shoulder from her ponytail. Today she wore a loose pale-yellow skirt and flowing white blouse. Maxi was dressing more casual lately. Maybe her bank-president husband—whom Claire suspected influenced Maxi's typically more formal appearance—was loosening up. It was about time.

"Her coffee must be cold by now." Claire touched the cup, finding it lukewarm beneath her fingers. "I'll go refresh this. I'm sure she'll be here any minute."

Claire brought the mug inside. The cafe was busy—customers sipping coffees, working on laptops, reading the papers. She waved to her regulars, Harry and Bert, who were seated at their usual table in the corner. And to think that just a few weeks ago the place had been flooded, and she'd feared she would be out of business.

Thankfully *that* didn't happen. Rob Bradford, who had opened the bread store across the street, had saved the day. Ironic, too, because at first Claire had feared that Bradford Breads would put her out of business. But it had all worked out, and luckily Ralph Marchand had been able to replace all the pipes in her shop in record time. Though the free pastries she'd supplied him with every day might have helped with that.

Hailey, her assistant, gave Claire a perky smile and brushed away some of the hair haphazardly falling into her face. "We just got an order for a sandcastle cake to be delivered Saturday. I quoted the usual price." Hailey referred to Claire's signature confection—a cake built from hand-cut cake layers shaped like a sandcastle and frosted with sugar-coated fondant that resembled sand.

"Great. I'll take a look at the order in a bit." Claire passed the mug over the counter to Hailey. "Would you mind dumping this and refilling it? Jane's late, and it got cold."

"Of course." Hailey took the mug cheerfully.

Hailey was really more than just an assistant. In fact, Claire didn't know what she'd do without her. Claire was grateful the plumbing issue hadn't affected Hailey. She was a single mother with a daughter to support. But that had been mostly due to Rob. He'd seen a way for Hailey to help them both out and earn more money at it too, though Claire knew the extra money Rob was paying her was due more to his generous heart than the extra work. But she was happy Hailey could make more. The girl deserved it.

Claire owed a lot to Rob. She snuck a peek across the street hoping to catch a glimpse of him inside his store and couldn't keep the smile off her face. Though they'd started off with a business relationship, it had turned into much more. A pang of guilt shot through her as she thought about Jane and Maxi.

Was it wrong that her life seemed to have come together in an unexpected but wonderful way while her friends appeared to be having problems?

"Here's Jane's coffee, just the way she likes it." Hailey held out the mug.

"Thanks." Claire took the mug, looked toward Bradford Breads one more time, wiped the silly smile off her face, and then headed back outside.

She and Jane reached the table at the same time. "Brought you a fresh coffee. How's your mom?"

"She's doing great, actually." Jane hugged Claire, then Maxi, and sat down, pulling the mug in front of her. "Sorry I'm late. Sandee came by the inn."

Claire made a face.

"Yech," Maxi said.

"I know. I had asked Dorian Wells to see how much Tides was worth—you know, just in case—and it turns out she's sick so I got Sandee. I told her to take a hike, though. Turns out selling Tides isn't going to help me out."

"You didn't want to sell anyway, did you?" Maxi asked.

Jane stared into her mug. "I promised my mother that I wouldn't, but I'm not sure I'm cut out for running an inn. Besides, it's expensive to keep Mom at Tall Pines, and now I've found out Medicaid won't cover her stay."

"Oh no." Claire pushed the plate with the chocolate chip muffin on it toward Jane.

Her friend picked at the wrapper mechanically, peeling it away from the muffin beneath one side at a time.

A bit distracted by something behind Claire, Maxi tore the top from the blueberry muffin that had been sitting in front of her while she sketched. "What do you mean? I thought you said your mother has no retirement savings to speak of."

"She doesn't. Apparently, she'd taken out all their retirement savings over the years to put into the inn."

"Can you pay for her to stay at Tall Pines?" Claire knew that business had been down at Tides. Jane had staff to pay, and if no one was staying there, how could she make enough?

"Well, that's what I need your help for. I need to figure out how to bring in more money at Tides. The place is in disrepair, and I have no idea how to attract customers." She stuffed another piece of muffin into her mouth, drowning out whatever else she had been about to say.

Maxi started clucking and cooing under her breath. With a frown, Claire twisted to look behind her. She spotted a shy tabby in the shadow of one of the potted plants, looking wary. Maxi waved a piece of her blueberry muffin, trying to entice the feline closer.

"Do cats even like blueberry muffins?" She might have better luck with a salmon muffin. Not that Claire thought she'd be able to sell one of those to anyone but a cat. And cats only paid in glares and disdainful flicks of their tails. At least that was what her own cat, Urchin, did.

"I guess we'll find out." Maxi wiggled the piece of muffin, but the cat continued to stare at her with uncertainty.

Jane swallowed the last of her chocolate chip muffin and chased it down with a sip of coffee. "This is really good, Claire. I missed these."

"I have my own kitchen back now, so I can bake the way I'm used to. It was nice of Rob to let me use his, but things just didn't seem to come out as good over there."

Jane teased, "You mean you weren't holding back out of fear that Rob would steal the recipe?"

"No, I've made them for Rob before."

Her two friends *oooh*ed like they were back in high school again. Maxi resumed waggling her fingers at the wary cat.

Claire willed the heat warming her cheeks away. She knew her friends were happy that she and Rob had connected, but the relationship still felt too new to talk about much. Claire steered away from the topic of her and Rob. "We were talking about Tides. What are you doing to get more customers?"

The teasing twinkle in Jane's eye flattened beneath the weight of the situation. "Not much, if I'm honest. Mom never did anything. Tourists always seemed to flock to the inn on their own. I know it's a bit run-down and that's part of the problem, but I'll have Sally do some fixes. The truth is I'm not sure what to do to get more people to stay there."

Maxi broke off another piece of muffin and waved it under the table. Absently, she said, "Why don't you do some of the things Claire was doing when she thought Bradford Breads was going to run her out of business?"

"I can text Tammi. She's an expert." As Claire spoke, she was already pulling her phone out of the pocket of her apron. "You probably can't have a three-for-one sale like I did, but you could put out some newspaper ads or get in touch with the radio station for an ad there. Awareness is half the battle. Maybe you aren't getting as many bookings because more people are using Airbnb. You have to do something to make Tides stand out."

Hope sparked in Jane's eyes. "It would be great if things picked up with ads. I mean, Tides is in a premium location on the beach. That would make it stand out, wouldn't it?"

Claire nodded as she typed a quick message into her phone and hit Send. "There. Tammi is probably sleeping right now, but I'll let you know what she says, and we can go from there."

Maxi cooed and clucked her tongue. "That's it, I'm not so scary."

Claire glanced over her shoulder to see that the tabby had tentatively emerged from the shadow of the potted plant. She tucked away her phone and frowned as she tried to think. "From what I remembered from when I asked her, she told me ads were big in the paper, but you also want to do things online. Have you kept the inn's website up to date?"

Jane opened her mouth then shut it again. She reached for the chocolate croissant on the plate in the center of the table. Her voice emerged as a squeak. "Website?"

"You must have a website," Claire said. "I had to

update mine. It only had one page with some pictures, but Tammi convinced me to have someone revamp it. It's not that expensive, but she said it's necessary."

Jane frowned. "I guess we have an old one too. Honestly, I haven't even looked at it in ages."

Claire whipped out her phone again, this time texting Jane. "I'm passing along the names of three web designers I got for mine. I ended up using Rachel Sanders. She was booked a few months out, so you might not want to wait for her. The others seemed good too."

"Great, thanks." Jane was trying to sound in control but looked overwhelmed.

"Aha! There you are, you handsome fellow." Triumphant, Maxi leaned down and scooped the cat into her lap. For a moment, it stood stiff and wary, but as she started to pet it, the cat settled into her and started to purr. Maxi smiled as she stroked the tabby's fur.

Claire couldn't help but smile too. "He knows how much you like cats." Maxi was forever monopolizing Urchin's attention whenever she came to visit Claire at her cottage, but Claire didn't mind. Maxi was clearly a cat lover. "You should get one of your own."

Although she continued to pander to the feline,

Maxi made a face. "James didn't seem too keen on that when I broached the subject before."

Claire seemed to remember something about James not wanting to get animal hair on his expensive suits.

"Sometimes you have to think about what *you* want, Maxi. I used to think only about what Peter wanted, and look where it got me. A big fat divorce and an ex with a snarky younger wife! I'm much better off now."

"Yes, but Peter never treated you right," Maxi pointed out. "It isn't the same with James at all. He's thinking about his career, a career he has used to keep us comfortable enough so that I could stay home and raise the kids. Other parents both had to work."

She had a point about the differences. James wasn't a bad guy, but at some point, one had to live their dream, and she was certain Maxi wasn't living hers.

Gently, she told Maxi, "Thinking about myself for a change has been what has gotten me to this point in my life. Look what I have now! I have something of my own, something I've always wanted to do. I'm living my dream life." Claire was proud of the way her life had turned out. Proud of the way she had picked up the pieces after her divorce and been selfish, for once in her life.

She honestly thought that it was high time for Maxi to be a little selfish too.

Maxi nodded. "Yeah, maybe you're right. But James is loosening up, and things take time. I'm working on him about a pet."

"Speaking of pets," Jane said. "I ran into this adorable golden retriever while I was at Tall Pines earlier. His name is Cooper, and he plowed me right over! I fell into a bush." She laughed, the color rising in her cheeks the only indication that she was a little self-conscious in the retelling.

"He sounds charming," Claire said, recognizing the twinkle in Jane's eye, even though it had been a while since she'd seen it. When she spoke of the dog, she all but glowed. And why shouldn't she? Dogs were in a perpetually good mood. Dogs followed their owners as though they were starved for attention, and they gave as much affection in return. Perhaps Maxi wasn't the only one of them who needed a pet. Jane had been a widow for a long time, and now that she didn't have her mother at home, a dog might be a great way to fill that hole.

Claire exchanged a glance with Maxi, who seemed to be thinking the same thing. It had been so long since Jane had allowed herself to care for someone else. From the time her son had died a decade ago, she'd been reluctant to let anyone new into her life in more than a superficial way. And now that her husband was gone, it must be lonely.

Rather than broach the subject just yet, Maxi asked, "Have you heard from Andrea?"

Jane's expression turned dark, but she shrugged as if she didn't care. "I've tried calling her to talk, but she hasn't called me back. We've exchanged a few texts, but I think the situation is too involved to get into with text messages. Either she'll call me to talk about it or she won't hear the details."

"Oh. Well, I hope she calls," Claire said.

Jane nodded. "Either way, I'm not sure she'll be much help. Speaking of which…" Jane picked her bag up from beside her chair and pushed up from the table. "I'd better get going. Lots to do."

Claire stood too. "Wait. I packaged up a chocolate chip muffin for Addie. I know you, and you'll be checking on her every night until you know she's settled in."

"Thanks, Claire. You're a good friend. I really appreciate it."

Claire hugged her tight, letting her know without words how much she was there to support Jane whenever she needed it. She ran in the cafe and grabbed the white bag with the Sandcastles logo. "Here. And give her my best when you see her."

"I will."

Still pinned in the chair beneath the stray cat, Maxi suggested, "Why don't we meet up for drinks later this evening at Splash? Tammi will have texted back by then, don't you think?"

Claire nodded. "I'm sure she'll have something for me to send along by then. What do you say, Jane?"

"That sounds really nice, actually."

"Then it's settled," Claire said with satisfaction. She hugged her friend one last time and whispered, "See you later."

Maxi reluctantly put the tabby down. The cat was well groomed. Its fur was sleek and soft, and it appeared to be well fed. She—or he—probably belonged to somebody, and it wasn't like Maxi could take it home anyway.

She helped Claire clean up the table and carried half the plates and cups back inside the bakery. She was happy that Claire had reopened, and not only because their weekly breakfasts together could now resume. The last month had been especially tough on Maxi for no good reason. After all, she wasn't dealing with the stress of redoing the pipes in her business or of balancing a business she barely knew with caring for an ailing mother like her two friends were. No, Maxi had the freedom to do whatever she wanted.

Well, *almost* whatever she wanted. Her mind turned to the hoard of sketchbooks she kept in the bench at the end of her bed. She hadn't mentioned to James that she'd kept those after giving up on sketching shortly after she'd had their first child. She sensed he didn't approve of her taking up the hobby again, as if painting and sketching didn't befit a bank president's wife. Maxi loved James with all her heart, but sometimes she didn't love the way he'd changed with all the responsibility of his position at the bank.

"Hey, Maxi, I'll take those." Hailey Robinson reached for the plates with a smile. Maxi had taken a liking to the young mother and she, Jane, and Claire thought of themselves as pseudo-grandmothers for Hailey's twelve-year-old daughter, Jennifer.

"How's Jennifer? Enjoying the summer, I hope." Maxi handed the plates off.

"She's great. She loved that kite you gave her. Uses it all the time. Why don't you come down to the beach sometime and help her fly it?"

"I might just do that," Maxi said. At least it would give her something to do, and James might even approve. Hailey disappeared into the kitchen, and

Maxi turned to Claire. "Can I have an almond scone to go?"

"Still hungry?" Claire eyed her as she opened the pastry case. "You ate two muffins."

Maxi laughed. "It's for later. I was thinking about taking a sketchbook up to the Marginal Way and doing a pencil sketch of the ocean."

"Really? That's great! You haven't done that since we were kids. I'm glad you're progressing from napkin sketches," Claire joked as she plucked a bakery tissue out of a box and reached into the case.

"Well, it's just a way to pass the time. I found an old sketchbook and figured I'd fill out the pages. Just for fun."

"You are a talented artist. You could make something out of it if you wanted. When we were kids, you always said you wanted to be an artist when you grew up."

Maxi remembered that desire well. It was like a rope of regret tugging at her even now. "Well, that wasn't a very practical ambition, and I'm not really *that* good."

Claire slipped the scone into a white bag and folded the top shut. "I'm sure you're better than you think. Your napkin sketches are lovely, and we're all our own worst critic, aren't we?"

Maxi mustered a faint smile. She reached into her purse to pay for the scone. Although Claire would have given it to her for free, it was important to Maxi to support her friend financially by buying the pastries she took home with her.

Claire handed the bag over the counter but kept hold of one end when Maxi grabbed for it. Gently, she said, "It might be good for you to take art up more seriously now that you've become an empty nester. How are you adjusting to that now?"

Maxi had shared her feelings with Claire and Jane when her youngest had gone off to college last year. After years of taking kids to sports events, doing laundry, and making sure the kitchen was supplied with snacks and meals, it was a bit of an adjustment. "It's a change, but I guess I'm getting used to it."

"It is a big change. Especially for the couples involved. How's James taking it?"

Maxi shrugged. "He seems okay. He works a lot, but that is usual, so we're doing fine."

She kept on a cheerful face for Claire, but there were times when she wondered if the kids had provided a bond for her and James that was no longer there. Things between them were different now. Of course, there were times when he was sweet and considerate just like he had been when they'd first been married. But then there were times when he worked such late hours that he came home only to eat and sleep.

Maxi paid for the scone, then tucked the bag with the scone into her large, striped tote bag for safekeeping. Not wanting to burden her friend with her problems, she changed the subject. "Did you see the way Jane's face lit up when she was talking about that dog?"

She and Claire moved to the side as another customer approached the cash register. Hailey took over to serve the customer, leaving Claire free to continue their chat.

"I did," Claire answered. "If you ask me, what Jane needs is a pet."

"It might help her during this transition time with her mom and the inn."

"You would do well with a pet too," Claire added. "But for different reasons. Jane is…" Her expression grew somber. "Jane is hurt. She needs to ease her way into opening up."

Maxi nodded. "I know. I can't imagine losing a child and a husband, and I know it still hurts her."

"If she only had a cat or a dog to open her heart to, I think she'd be much closer to healing. I'm afraid she's shutting too many doors and missing out on life."

Maxi adjusted the straps of her tote bag higher on

her shoulder. "You think she should find a new boyfriend?"

"Not necessarily. Just because I did doesn't mean it's for everybody. But if Jane decides to remain single, I think it should be because her life is full without a romantic partner, not because she's afraid of losing someone again."

"It would also help if her sister came back. I remember that Jane idolized her once, but I don't think they've been close since Andie left for college. Do you know why she hardly ever visits?"

Looking weary, Claire shook her head. "Not really. I got the impression that Lobster Bay was just too small for her. I guess her dreams were too big to fit in the town. It's too bad."

Maxi noticed her friend's gaze drift toward the front window of the bakery, which overlooked Bradford Breads across the street.

Dreamily, Claire added, "This town is the perfect size for me. It always has been."

"Especially now," Maxi teased.

Claire didn't seem to notice, still staring across the street. Maxi smiled. Claire was smitten. And judging by the look on Rob's face every time Maxi had seen him and Claire together, the feeling was mutual. It was so warming to see, especially after everything Claire had been through.

"You're right. Lobster Bay has always been perfect for me too. I never even thought of leaving, except maybe to go to college." But Maxi's dreams had included art school in Paris, not a math degree from Massachusetts. In the end, she hadn't even used the degree, but she had a beautiful home and three wonderful children. She couldn't complain about any of that. "Well, I better run. I'll see you tonight."

CHAPTER 5

*B*y midafternoon, Jane was sick of numbers. She'd gone over the books twice, set up an appointment with Shane Flannery, and sent messages to the web designers whose contact info Claire had given her. She was starting to think that maybe she could make this work.

She took a break to walk on the beach. Strolling at the edge near the surf, she watched for interesting shells. It was just past high tide, and you never knew what treasures the ocean might have left. A brown, striped spiral shell tumbled in the foamy surf, and she bent to pick it up. Some type of whelk or conch shell, she wasn't sure. It was pretty common, and she had bowls full of them. Jane only kept the rare shells these days, so she tossed it back, the motion helping to loosen the stiff muscles in her neck.

She stretched, bringing her arms over her head, and turned away from the ocean. This part of the beach was practically deserted because there were no public parking lots nearby. It was dotted with quaint cottages that were painted in pretty colors—aqua, pink, mint green.

Wait. Was that Sandee Harris in the window of one of those cottages? Jane would recognize that bleach-blond haircut anywhere. Sandee was the last person she wanted to talk to. Hopefully she wouldn't look this way. It was kind of hard to hide out in the middle of the beach.

But Sandee *didn't* look at the beach. She was too focused on the man next to her, a man whose arm she was leaning over as she showed him something invisible from Jane's vantage point. That wasn't…

James? *Maxi's husband?* It couldn't be. He never took off his suit jacket. But his profile was familiar. What was he doing with Sandee? Maxi hadn't said anything about investing in a cottage, particularly one so close to home. Maybe Jane was mistaken. She needed a closer look.

As she started toward the cottage, the pair moved

out of sight, away from the back window and into another room.

Weird. Maxi had always said she wanted to have a cottage on the beach where she could paint all day. Maybe they were finally buying one. But Jane had just seen Maxi this morning, and she hadn't mentioned a thing.

A bark gave her thirty seconds of warning before a golden ball of fur launched into her. The next thing she knew, she was lying in the sand, an eager golden retriever nose stuck in her face right before his tongue lapped her cheek.

"Cooper! Come here!"

Jane laughed, further encouraging Cooper, who wagged his entire body. She balled her hands in his fur, trying to pat him and push him away at the same time. She had to admit the exuberant devotion of the dog felt good. That was something you sure didn't get from people.

"Cooper." Mike sounded exasperated this time and much nearer. A moment later, Cooper jumped off Jane.

She rose up on her elbows and caught her breath before Mike's charming smile appeared in front of her face as he battled the dog one-handed and offered her the other.

"We have to stop meeting like this."

She smiled back at him. "One of these days I would like to be upright when we meet." Her voice was a little breathless. She took his hand, letting him help her to stand before she started to brush off the sand as best she could.

Cooper divided his attention between them, his tail moving back and forth in a perpetual wag.

"Here, boy," Mike said, swiping a stick of driftwood off the beach. "Fetch!"

Cooper looked conflicted as he glanced between Jane and Mike. However, when Mike let the stick fly, the dog rocketed down the beach after it.

"Are you all right?" Mike asked, his eyes twinkling.

Jane couldn't help but notice that in addition to a nice smile, Mike also had nice eyes. When she'd met him in front of Tall Pines, she'd thought them gray or brown. But here, in the sunlight, they looked green. A beautiful shade of green that reminded her of the ocean. Why in the world was she noticing these things about him?

"I'm fine," she answered, her voice even quieter than usual. She glanced at the beach to see that Cooper, unable to find his initial stick of driftwood, had found an even bigger piece and was on his way back, carrying it precariously. When she risked a glance toward Mike, she found him watching her with that smile still in place.

"Did your grandfather live here on the beach?" Jane gestured back toward the cottages. "I remember you said you were staying here to care for him."

"Actually, I'm renting one of the cottages. I was staying at Gramps's place over on Elm Street, but it sold last week."

Something felt sad and final about Mike's grandfather's place being sold, as if he could never go back. Though clearly Addie could never go back, either, especially not if Jane screwed up and didn't get Tides profitable again. That would be doubly problematic since there would be no Tides for Addie to go back to and also no money to keep her at Tall Pines.

Mike must have sensed her thoughts. His eyes were sad as he watched Cooper. "It was kind of a bummer letting the old place go. Gramps loved living in the town. He used to be a town official here."

"You know, I think I might remember my grandparents mentioning a George Henderson. Is that your grandfather?" Jane asked.

"Yep. They probably knew each other. Seems like most people in town did back then."

Cooper dropped the stick proudly at Mike's feet. It was as big around as Mike's fist and nearly as long as the dog. Mike stared blankly at it. "What do you expect me to do with that?"

The dog sat proudly, his tail thumping the sand.

With a sigh, Mike bent to pick up the stick. "This thing has to weigh ten pounds!"

He threw the stick hard, and Cooper took off after it.

"I'm sure your grandfather appreciates you being here and taking Cooper to see him. Will you stay out here long?"

"I'm a programmer. I can work on my code from anywhere, but I'll have to go back at some point." Mike's face turned serious as he looked down at Cooper, who had returned with a different stick. "I'm not sure what I'll do with Cooper, though. My apartment in Seattle is definitely not dog friendly."

Jane's heart pinched as images of Cooper sad and depressed in a small apartment—or worse, inside a cage at the animal shelter—bubbled up. A dog like Cooper needed room to run.

Mike picked the stick up and threw it. "But I guess I'll figure something out. He's a good dog, deserves a good home. Besides, I'm not ready to leave yet. Gramps needs me."

"Well, they're both lucky to have you," Jane said. "I

guess I better get back. My inn is down at the other end of the beach."

"Oh, well, then I guess I'll see you around?"

"Probably," she said as she turned to leave.

When she glanced behind her, she found Mike shading his eyes, keeping a closer watch over Cooper. The dog was happily frolicking in the waves, chasing them up and down the beach. Jane couldn't help but laugh.

And just like that, the tension melted from her body, and she wished that she could stay. Because the dog, for whatever reason, made her forget the weight of her worries, the weight of the past. She could just be herself, free and happy.

But she couldn't stay. She had lots to do to rebuild Tides. After a moment, she turned back and continued to the inn.

Mike tore his gaze away from the happily frolicking dog to watch Jane walk away, his mind automatically comparing her to the last woman he'd dated, Tiffany. She was the complete opposite. Of course, he wasn't dating Jane, not even close. He barely knew her, but he wouldn't mind getting to know her a little better.

Though maybe dating wasn't a good idea. The last relationship had not gone well. He should have listened to his best friend about dating a woman six years younger than him, even if she was thirty-five. She acted more like twenty-five and was prone to drama, not the least of which was the way she refused to accept the fact that things were over between them.

Jane was more mature, and she didn't seem the least bit like a drama queen. She fit with Lobster Bay—humble, unassuming, peaceful. She was elegant in a way most woman strived to be. The short haircut, that might look mannish on some women, looked incredibly feminine on her. She didn't wear a lot of makeup or color her hair like Tiffany had either. Nor did she dress in tight flashy clothes designed to draw the eye—but classy, plain clothing that made a man feel at ease while still admiring her figure. Jane had a nice figure, long legs and a lean body that told him this wasn't the only time he'd find her walking along the beach. Maybe, if he was lucky, she'd do it daily.

Judging by the age of her mother at Tall Pines and what she'd said, she might be a bit older than him, but probably not by much. What was a few years between them at their age, anyway? Besides, she was cute, and he liked the way she blushed every time she fiddled with her hair. If he gave her just the right smile, he got that faint blush in return. It had become a challenge.

Yes, he definitely hoped to see her again.

His eyes flew to Cooper just as the dog plunged into a particularly deep wave then bounded back onto the beach, shaking the water off and looking toward Mike.

Mike sighed and rubbed his hand over the back of his neck. The dog needed more than his small apartment. The longer Mike spent in his company, the more attached he became, even though he knew it wouldn't be fair to the dog to cart him back to Seattle. He'd have to find a home for the dog here, but it was going to be hard to leave him. Cooper had such a good personality.

Honestly, it was going to be difficult for Mike to leave Gramps too. Some of his fondest memories had been made on the coast of Maine: Gramps teaching him how to fish. Tagging along at Gramps's heels as they visited the community, helping people out who needed it. Mike had spent most of his summers around this area, a world away from his parents' suburban home. Returning made him feel lighter, carefree.

But he couldn't stay. His life was in Seattle.

Or was it? What did he have back home that he couldn't have right here? He was forty-one years old, and all of his friends were married with children. Most of their time was spent with their kids. He'd broken up with Tiffany. He could telecommute. Truth was, he really didn't have much back in Seattle, and Gramps needed someone nearby as his power of attorney.

Mike's phone pinged, and he slipped it out of his pocket to check it out of habit. Tiffany. Scowling, he shoved it back in. That was, what? The sixth text he'd received from her in the past two days? He'd taken to counting them, responding only to every fourth. He should block her and stop replying, but he didn't want to be rude. It might have to come to that, though. The girl just was not getting the message, even though he had spelled it out as plain as day the last time they'd talked in person.

Tiffany was one more reason to stay here, to start fresh. As he glanced down the beach after Jane's retreating figure, he turned over the idea in his mind. He didn't have any reason to go back to Seattle, except for the cactuses on his windowsill. The idea of staying here, in Lobster Bay, was becoming more appealing the longer he thought about it.

CHAPTER 6

*J*ane returned to Tides in time to snag the last remaining lemon poppy seed muffin, see Brenda out the door, and vigorously clean the sunroom. The part-time maid had dusted and laundered the bedsheets from Mrs. Weatherlee's room. With no other guests, there wasn't much else for her, or Jane, to do. Jane checked the messages on the answering machine, but no new bookings had come in, so she retreated to the rocking chair on the porch with her muffin and a cup of coffee.

Rocking in the chair, her thoughts turned to Cooper. The dog was a welcome distraction from her troubles, and she leaned forward and craned her neck to see if she could spot him down the beach. She couldn't, though. The section in front of the cottages was too far away, but it was nice to think she might run into Cooper again, simply by walking down that way. She'd run into Mike, too, but it was Cooper she really wanted to see, of course.

Jane settled back in the chair and fished her cell phone out of her pocket, taking in a deep breath to steel herself before dialing her sister. Andrea had returned her call earlier, but she'd missed it. Now it was time to call her back. Too bad all she got was voicemail.

Jane sighed. "I guess I missed you again. Call me later." She hung up, not knowing what else to say.

She stuffed a big bite of muffin into her mouth and opened the email app on her phone. She had a lot to accomplish and no idea where to start except to see if someone had gotten back to her about the website work she needed done.

Only one of the website designers she'd emailed had answered her, and the news wasn't favorable.

Hi, Jane. I'd be happy to redesign your website, but I'm booked solid for the next three months. I can start working on it then, if that timeline works for you. Let me know, and I'll give you a quote.

Three months! No, that timeline did not work for Jane. For all she knew, by then she might be out of business. Luckily there were two other web designers. Surely one of them would be able to start sooner.

They had to because she needed a better website. But, of course, that wouldn't help if she didn't start tending to some of the maintenance issues at Tides. She closed her eyes, rocking in sync with the waves as she made a mental list of the things that needed to be spruced up. First there were the railings on the stairs that needed repair, the wallpaper in the sunroom, the molding in the front parlor needed to be painted—

"Is this a bad time?" Sally's voice permeated her thoughts.

"No, sorry. I was just thinking. Are you done for the day?"

"Your windows are all tight as can be. There won't be any cold air coming in through cracks this year. That, I promise."

"Thank you. I really appreciate you fixing up the inn so quickly." Not everyone was willing to go to such lengths to make time for her, and she didn't want Sally to get overwhelmed with all the work ahead of her. "I spoke to Shane Flannery, and he's coming for an interview."

Sally nodded approvingly. "He's a good sort. Loyal. Hardworking."

"I know," Jane said simply.

"You know him?"

She shrugged. "We went to high school together. He and my sister dated for a long time."

"Oh, that's right. I think I remember that now." Sally studied her for a few seconds. "Is something bothering you?"

Jane sighed. "I was just going over all the things that need to be done to get Tides in tip-top shape so we can bring in more customers. It's overwhelming."

"Ah-yuh," Sally said, with feeling. "I can see it would be. But don't worry, once you get Shane on board, the two of us can whip it into shape. This place has charm, but if you got with the times and modernized it a bit, I'm sure you'd have people coming here in droves."

Jane stopped rocking in the chair and tilted her head, thinking.

"What do you mean?"

Sally shrugged. "You need to do something to make it stand out from those Airbnbs cropping up everywhere. Talk about the delicious breakfasts you make here—Brenda offered me a piece of quiche when I got in earlier. I'd stay here just for that! And why don't you have some tables out here so your customers can come out and watch the ocean while they eat? It would be perfect."

Jane considered her words in silence. Neither her

grandparents nor her parents had served meals on the porch, but nowadays restaurants all had outdoor seating. She'd just gotten used to doing things the way they'd always been done and only serving in the dining room. Sally might be on to something.

With a sigh, Sally shook her head. "Has your sister given you a reason why she hasn't come down to help you run this place?"

"We've been playing phone tag, but I suppose she's busy. She has a very demanding job as an antiques appraiser at Christie's in New York." Why did she feel the need to defend Andie?

Sally made a face. "Ah-yuh, I know. Fancy city job. That girl always did want more than she had. But the thing she never realized is that sometimes you've already got what you really need. They say 'Home is where the heart is' for a reason."

Jane looked out over the ocean. "I know exactly what you mean."

It was part of why she *couldn't* sell the inn. Not without taking her best shot at running it first. Every time she walked through the door, she was comforted by happy memories. "But I'm not sure Andie will ever realize that. I don't think she feels the same way we do about Lobster Bay."

Sally *tsk*ed under her breath. "I wouldn't be so sure of that. Home calls to us all at some point."

Maybe Andie had made herself a home away from Lobster Bay. Maybe she was happy. Jane didn't really know because they'd grown apart over the decades. They'd never gotten back to the closeness they'd had when they were younger, and somehow over the years, Jane had stopped hoping it would magically happen.

Jane looked out over the beach and then back at the inn. Sure, it might need a coat of paint and there might be a few broken things here and there, but Tides was her family legacy, and Jane was going to do her best to make it profitable again, whether or not her sister cared to be a part of it.

•

ndie poked her head into Doug's office.

"Fancy finding you here," she said with a little laugh. She meant the statement to be ironic, poking fun at the fact that too often when she had stepped past this same office in the last week, Doug *hadn't* been inside. She'd thought he'd been avoiding her. Maybe he'd only been busy.

She stepped into the office. Doug had always been messy. It was in direct contrast with his neatly trimmed beard threaded with silver and the suits and ties or sweater vests he tended to wear to the office. But as much as the clutter of his office sometimes got on Andie's nerves, it was also kind of charming in a distracted-professor sort of way.

She trailed her fingers over the edge of the desk as

she waited for him to look at her. "When did you get back in? I didn't realize you'd come back."

"Is there something you need? I'm really busy."

His voice was curt, and it cut her. She gritted her teeth, trying not to show it. She'd feel better if he looked like a mess, stressed up to his eyeballs or over-worked and exhausted. But no, he looked pristine. Cold and pristine.

She could take a hint, even if it stung.

She should have known she would get hurt if she carried on with a married man. A part of her had hated it—and herself—from the start. It was why she pushed him about the divorce. She'd wondered all along if the separation was really as final as he'd said. But now she was starting to wonder if maybe his lack of attention had more to do with a certain new employee than it had to do with his not really wanting to make the break from his wife.

Well, the heck with him.

"I need time off," she blurted out.

He frowned. He pulled the reading glasses off his nose and tossed them haphazardly onto the desk. How he'd be able to find them again in the pile of all that junk was anybody's guess. "You can submit a vacation request."

"Actually, I need time off now. Today. I finished my

cataloguing for today, and I have a family emergency at home."

His eyebrows climbed. "I didn't know anyone in your family was sick."

If he'd even remotely listened to her, he would have known about her mother's health problems. But Doug had always been all about himself. Tightly, she told him, "There's been a decline in my mom's health, and I have to go home."

"Home is... where?"

"Lobster Bay. It's in Maine."

He grunted. Why wasn't he consoling her? She didn't expect him to leap over the desk or anything, especially not here at work where everyone could see, but a few friendly words would have been nice.

"That's a long way from here. What if the Rich-haven estate comes up while you're away?"

"Text me if that happens, and I'll fly back."

He was treating her like she was a new, flaky employee, not a woman he'd known and dated for the past few years. When they'd started their affair, she had felt as though he had seen her, valued her. Now it was clear he didn't.

But maybe, if she left, he would. Not as a girlfriend —now that she was seeing another side of him, she realized that she'd known for quite some time their relationship was going nowhere. And oddly, it didn't hurt as much as it should have. Maybe she'd dated him because deep down she knew he would never be able to make things more permanent.

She hadn't been satisfied for months with their arrangement, and he didn't care enough about her to keep her happy. Besides, didn't she deserve somebody who gave her his full attention, who didn't keep her as his dirty little secret?

"Okay, fair enough. If it's an emergency, you must go, then."

"I'll call you later in the week and let you know how long I think this emergency will take. Text or email me if the Richhaven estate comes up. Goodbye, Doug."

She turned and walked out of the room, feeling lighter for having turned her back on him. She needed to get away—from all of this, but especially from Doug. And maybe, with her gone, he'd realize how big of an asset she was to this company.

After all, no kid barely out of college could do her job like Andie could. It was about time somebody acknowledged that.

CHAPTER 8

The sun was just about to set when Jane arrived at Splash, the oceanside restaurant that she, Claire, and Maxi frequented. Splash was casual, with an outdoor eating area on the beach. Tiny white lights twinkled from the umbrellas, and frothy waves washed up on the beach in front of them. The evening sky reflected the pinks and blues of the sunset.

Maxi and Claire where already seated with drinks in front of them. Maxi's had a tiny plastic pink mermaid perched on the rim—Claire's, a blue seahorse. Jane ordered a salty seafarer margarita and sat in the empty chair facing the ocean.

"We put in an order of steamers." Claire glanced over the rim of her drink. "How are things going at the inn? Any new bookings or ideas?"

"Not too bad. I'm going to hire Sean Flannery to help Sally so we can get some repairs done." Jane's drink came, and she took a sip, glancing out at a dog frolicking on the beach. It reminded her of Cooper, and she smiled, craning her neck toward the end of the beach where the cottages were. But of course the section where Cooper lived was way too far down.

"Looking for someone?" Maxi asked.

Jane blushed. "No, I just ran into that dog again on the beach. Cooper, the one I told you about?"

Maxi and Claire glanced at each other, and Jane caught a look between them. What was that about? Thinking about Cooper and Mike reminded her that she also thought she'd seen James. "I guess he is staying up in those cottages at the north end. Did you say you were looking into buying one of those, Maxi?"

Maxi scrunched her face. "What? Buy a cottage? No. Why would we do that?"

Jane was confused. Maxi wouldn't lie to her, and she seemed surprised by the question. The man probably hadn't been James at all. Plenty of men were his height with dark hair. Jane glanced down at her drink. "No reason. I thought you mentioned that a while ago, and the cottages there are adorable. Very artsy."

"So, this guy you met at Tall Pines and his dog live there?" Claire asked.

"Just renting, I guess. He's from Seattle and just here to get his grandfather settled at Tall Pines." Jane looked from the beach to her friends. "I told you guys this before, didn't I?"

"You did. Having a dog is always nice. I wish I could have a pet." Maxi looked out at the beach wistfully.

"I have Urchin, but he doesn't run on the beach. The only place he runs to is his food bowl," Claire joked.

Maxi laughed. "You could have a dog at Tides, Jane. A mascot for the inn."

"I don't know. Not everyone likes dogs." The idea wasn't totally unappealing. She'd always wanted a dog as a kid, but her parents had said that the inn was no place for pets. But that had been forty years ago. Times had changed, and now dogs were welcomed everywhere. Even the local restaurants were starting to allow them. Jane filed that away for future thought. She had more important things to talk about. "I'm dying to know if you heard from Tammi. Did she have any marketing advice? I really need to get on this."

"Yes, as a matter of fact, she had some great suggestions." Claire paused as the waitress slid a large white bowl filled to the brim with steamed clams onto the table then set down another for the shells and a few small bowls of broth and butter. "She suggested advertising in papers, but not local, of course. You need to go to the big cities people will want to get away from for a seaside vacation."

"That makes sense. What else?" Jane grabbed a shell and peeled the clam out. She swirled it in the broth then the butter then popped it in her mouth.

"She suggested some getaway specials, especially in the slow season." Claire picked through the bowl, coming up with one of the larger clams.

"Every season is slow lately. Did she suggest anything I could do now?"

"Well, you need a website first and foremost, but you're already working on that." Claire tossed her shells in the discard bowl and dug for another clam.

"I've only heard back from one of them so far, and they can't do it for three months."

"Three months! That won't work. Tammi said a website with a way to book online is critical these days. No one wants to call anymore. She looked at your website and said it's outdated, and a contact page with just an email and phone number won't do." Claire dipped her clam in the butter. "And she said you need to get set up on Google and Yelp and all that."

"You might want to check with the chamber of commerce here. I think they have a website with all the local businesses listed. Might be good to get on there with a link to your site," Maxi added.

"Hopefully one of the other website designers will reply soon. Maybe I should email them again." Jane would definitely need help with the website. She was technically challenged. "What else?"

"She mentioned something about a unique selling proposition, you know, something that sets Tides apart," Claire said.

"Sort of like your sandcastle cakes set your bakery apart?" Jane asked.

"Exactly!"

"Sally suggested doing things that make the inn more appealing, like maybe having tables set up on the back porch for dining. But lots of places have that now. I don't know if it's unique enough."

"That's a great idea." Maxi sipped her drink. "Oh! Maybe you could have a special event out there. Like maybe a wine tasting or something?"

"Hmm... I like that train of thought. That might bring in a bit of money, but we'd have to make it something really big to entice people to stay overnight," Jane said.

"Maybe you could offer some sort of package," Claire said.

"It would be great if we could combine a money-making event with a reason for guests to stay over." Jane was starting to feel hopeful.

Maxi snapped her fingers "I've got it! You could do beach weddings."

Jane frowned. "Weddings? I don't know anything about putting on a big wedding. Seems like that could lead to disaster."

"Not big weddings, small niche weddings." Maxi was on a role, her gestures animated. "The beach wedding could be your unique selling point, at least for weddings."

Claire jumped in, just as excited. "And weddings bring in a lot of money."

Jane appreciated that her friends were excited for her, but all she felt was anxiety. This wasn't something she could pull off, was it? She'd never done anything like this before. "But it would take permits, and we'd have to have it catered, and need tents and a dance floor—"

Maxi put her hand on Jane's arm. "All things that are easy to do. Think about it. We have the tent-rental place right in town, and there are plenty of good caterers. Claire could make sandcastle wedding cakes. Lots of people would want a wedding like this."

"And who would deny you a permit? Your family

has been a mainstay in the town for generations. Everyone wants you to succeed," Claire assured her.

"It would be guaranteed bookings since the whole wedding party would want to stay at Tides." Maxi sat back and sipped her drink. "You could take out an ad in *Niche Wedding Magazine*. My daughter-in-law scoured that thing to find a good wedding venue for their wedding."

"I suppose it might work. Mom's gardens have gotten overgrown, but we could spruce those up and put the dance floor next to them. Sally could probably build a portable one that we can store in the old garage." Jane glanced at the beach. "Maybe we could do a lobster bake right on the beach, you know, to set Tides apart."

"Now you're thinking," Claire said. "Why not take out an ad and see what happens? It could generate a huge influx of money."

"I don't know. I don't want to bite off more than I can chew, but I suppose I could send some feelers out." Jane sat back and sipped her drink, her mind reeling with possibilities. How much profit could a wedding bring in? She pushed down a wave of panic at the thought of taking on something so big. If this would help her save Tides, she'd have to step out of her comfort zone.

CHAPTER 9

The next morning, Jane woke to an email at the business address for Tides. She had a booking! She hadn't even put any of Tammi's suggestions into play, and already things were looking up.

She called the number in the email and talked to a pleasant man named Chandler Vanbeck. He was an art appraiser coming to town to scope locations for a new art gallery. He'd seen Tides on a previous trip. Jane happily booked him for the week and went downstairs.

Mrs. Weatherlee was seated in the dining room with her breakfast, and Jane swung in to exchange some pleasantries then went outside. She wanted to take a walk on the beach and think about the opportunities she'd talked about with Maxi and Claire at Splash.

Walking on the beach always helped her think things through.

She'd lain awake for most of the night, going back and forth on the idea of weddings. What if she booked a wedding and failed? It would be a risk, but it would bring in the most money and could be the thing that saved Tides. Of course, there was no guarantee that anyone would want to book the inn for a wedding. Maybe it would be better if she focused on smaller events like a wine tasting or clambake.

She slipped off her sandals and let the sand warm the bottoms of her feet as she walked down to the surf. She missed her sister. Even though they weren't close now, it would be nice to have someone to bounce ideas off of. Of course, she had Claire and Maxi, and they cared about her more than Andie did, it seemed. But Tides wasn't their family inn, it wasn't a part of them, and only Andie would know exactly how it felt to weigh these decisions. But maybe Andie didn't care about their family legacy like Jane did. Andie still hadn't returned her last call.

The freezing water of the Atlantic turned Jane's toes numb even in the heat of summer as she splashed in the froth at the waves' edge. She headed toward the north end of the beach, keeping her eye out for Cooper and Mike.

A ding from her phone signaled that she'd received an email on the Tides business account.

Another booking? She looked at her phone eagerly only to be disappointed. It was one of the web designers, this one replying to say that they were booked for four months. Shoot! Hopefully the third time would be the charm. She needed a website desperately, according to Tammi.

Her hopes dampened, she turned back. She didn't have time for a long walk, and she wanted to get started on researching what types of events she could have so she could get the ball rolling on setting them up. Would the efforts be a waste without a website? Claire had given her three names, and two were booked solid. She should probably look for more designers just in case the third was booked up too.

Her phone plinked, signaling a text message.

It was Andrea. She was flying in today, and she'd be here in the late afternoon. Jane hadn't expected her to come at all. And now she'd be coming to see Tides was run-down and had no guests. Suddenly the state of Tides felt like a reflection on Jane. Like she'd somehow fallen down on the job and was responsible for ruining the family business.

She started walking with purpose, suddenly realizing that more than anything she wanted to prove that she could revive Tides. As she walked back, she googled "niche weddings" and found the magazine Maxi had told her about. There was a form where you could apply to be listed as a niche wedding venue.

Squinting at the screen, she thumbed in the information. It asked for the usual basic info but also wanted to know anything that made the venue special or unique. Jane figured an old home with a gorgeous view of the ocean right on the beach was pretty special, so she took a picture of Tides, angling it to show off the wide porch and avoid the overgrown gardens. Then she turned and snapped a photo of the ocean. Later on she could add pictures of the guest rooms and dining room. None of these pictures were truly unique, though. What could she offer to make someone's wedding different? A thought occurred. She had one more photo she could add, and she was sure no other wedding venue would have anything like it. *That* photo she could only get at Sandcastles.

Her thumb hovered over the submit button for a few seconds, then she pressed it. Maybe she could make this work after all.

Sandcastles was bustling with customers, and Claire

was behind the counter cashing out a woman who was buying two boxes full of pastries when Jane arrived.

"I see business is good," Jane said.

"Yeah." Claire secured a strand of auburn hair into the clip on the back of her head. "I was afraid people would forget about this place when we were closed to repair the pipes, but I guess they didn't."

"I told you they wouldn't. Your stuff is too good to forget about." Jane glanced over at the case where Claire kept her signature sandcastle cakes. "Speaking of which, if I'm going to do weddings, I was thinking to make them really beachy. Maybe a lobster bake on the beach, and I thought that including your sandcastle cakes for the wedding cake would be something really unique. Would you make them for the weddings?"

"You decided to do weddings! That's great." Claire slipped out from behind the counter and walked over to the case with Jane. "Of course I'll make them."

"Good, I was thinking about taking a picture of one to submit to that magazine Maxi talked about." Jane held up her phone.

"Let me find a spot that will look good in a photo." Claire turned slowly. "How about this table in front of the window?"

"Perfect."

They took the cake out and arranged it on the table.

Harry and Bert, well-known regulars at Sandcastles, were seated beside the table, having their usual coffee and reading the paper.

"What's this about weddings? Are you having one at Tides?" Harry winked at Bert. "I hope Claire and Rob decided to get married?"

Claire blushed and swatted at Harry. "No. Jane is offering weddings at the inn."

Claire might have protested, but Jane could see she kind of liked the idea of marrying Rob. Of course, it was way too soon, but maybe someday she would be hosting Claire's wedding. It warmed her heart to see her friend so happy.

"Oh, that's a great idea. Such a pretty spot," Bert said.

"Who doesn't love a beach wedding?" Harry added.

"I think it will be a great way to expand business." Sally's voice drifted up from the floor. Jane hadn't seen her crouched there, painting the baseboard. "Tides is a beautiful venue for a wedding. I can just picture the back porch set up with tables, flower vases, candlelight, white linen cloths."

Jane smiled at her. "That's part of the plan. Of course, I'm also going to need some other things, like a dance floor."

"Oh, don't worry about that." Sally balanced the

brush on the top of the can and stood, wiping paint off her fingers with a cloth. "I can whip something up. You'll probably need an arbor for the happy couple to get married under. And I think we need to spruce up the common areas for guests to mingle inside. Well, with Shane helping, all that will be no problem."

"Great. I knew I could count on you." Jane warmed with the support of everyone, and now the task didn't feel so monumental.

"What's this I hear about a wedding?" The grating voice came from behind Jane. Sally's smile slipped.

Jane turned, and her own smile faded when she saw it was Sandee Harris. She hadn't even noticed her in here, the place had been so crowded. Why had she even come here? Was it to rub it in that she'd stolen Claire's husband? It was mean—just the sort of thing Sandee would do. Though Jane doubted Claire cared about that anymore. She had Rob now, and he was way better than Peter. So Sandee was the loser in this one.

"I'm thinking about having a wedding venue at Tides," Jane said.

"Oh?" Sandee's brows rose. "So you aren't going to sell the place? I'm surprised."

"No, we're going to try to revive it, bring it back to the way it was before my mom got sick," Jane said, the snooty look in Sandee's eyes only adding to her determination.

"Good luck. The place needs a lot, but I'm sure you can handle it." Sandee gave her a fake smile, her tone implying that she wasn't sure of that at all. She turned and left.

Jane turned back to Claire and Sally in time to see Sally stick her tongue out.

"That woman is bad news." Sally crouched again and picked up the brush then glanced at Jane over her shoulder. "I'll be out tomorrow, and we can talk about specifics."

"Great. Thanks."

Jane helped Claire put the cake back. Once it was safely in the case, Claire leaned against the side and crossed her arms over her chest. "Weddings are going to work out great. You'll see."

Jane held up crossed fingers. "Let's hope."

Claire's expression turned serious. "That's going to be a lot of work. If you need help, just shout. I know you'll be there all alone, and trying to run the inn and set up weddings could be a lot to take on by yourself."

"Thanks, but I won't exactly be all alone, at least not for the next few days. I just found out that Andie is coming."

"Oh, that's great. I'm sure she'll be a big help."

Jane held up crossed fingers again. "Again, let's hope."

Jane wasn't sure if Andie would be any help. She usually just breezed in and left quickly, but she had to admit that she would love it if her sister did help. Somewhere deep inside sprouted a seed of hope that their mother's illness and resurrecting Tides could bring her and Andie close again.

As she left Sandcastles, she called Maxi. If she was going to pull off this wedding venture, she was going to need some help decorating.

Maxi fluffed the pillow on her couch for the fifth time that morning. She stood back, arms crossed over her chest, surveying the arrangement.

Maybe if she put the two white pillows on the ends and the gray-and-black striped in the middle.

She turned away with a sigh. What did it matter? Rearranging the decor in the house was like taking a grain of sand from one side of the beach and putting it on the other. The house already looked great, but she was bored and didn't have much to do.

Her gaze fell on a family photo on the whitewashed hutch next to the stairs. She and James stood in the back, the three kids lined up in front of them. The kids had been small, ages five through ten. The picture brought up happy memories. She missed the sounds of kids running through the house, but this was the course of life, wasn't it? She cocked her head and looked toward the kitchen, picturing a dog or cat padding toward her. Not quite the same as a toddler, but a lot less work. Perfect for the stage of life she was at. Now if only she could get James on board.

She'd expected that the kids would eventually leave home, but what she hadn't expected was the way her relationship with James would change. She never anticipated that they would grow apart.

Maybe it was normal to go through some growing pains once the kids left the nest? She supposed she should give it more thought before she started to worry that something was wrong in their marriage.

She didn't get a chance to think about it too much because then her phone rang. It was Jane.

"Hi, Jane. What's up?" Jane rarely called. They usually texted. Maxi's heart fluttered. The last time Jane had called was when Addie had wandered away from Tides and gotten lost. Hopefully nothing was wrong.

"I hope I'm not bothering you, but I wanted to call and talk instead of texting."

"Is something wrong with your mom?"

"Oh. No, nothing like that. Nothing's wrong. Actually, I wanted to ask for your help."

"My help?" Maxi's spirits lifted. "With what?"

Maxi had helped decorate Addie's room, and she'd loved the challenge. Perhaps Jane wanted her input at the inn. Right about now any project would be exciting.

"I put in an application at that wedding website that you mentioned. And I was thinking if we're going to have weddings, I'm going to need some advice on how to decorate the place for them."

"That's wonderful!" Maxi couldn't be happier for her friend. She knew Jane sometimes liked to follow the safe path, but she had a feeling that hosting weddings and other events at Tides was going to help pull them through. And she really wanted Jane to pull Tides through, not only so that Addie could stay at Tall Pines but for Jane to feel like she'd accomplished something. "I'm happy to help with anything. Do you want to get together and talk about it in person?"

"I'd love to. I have to visit Mom this afternoon, and my sister is coming tonight. So I won't have time today, but would you mind coming over tomorrow around ten?"

"Mind? I'd love it."

Maxi made a cup of coffee and sat at her kitchen counter, her outlook brightening. Helping Jane with the weddings would give her a purpose, a goal. She'd had too much time on her hands lately, and maybe she'd been seeing problems where there were none. Hopefully having something to focus on other than her empty nest would prove that things at home weren't as bad as she'd thought.

CHAPTER 10

Jane's office at Tides was on the third floor. It was small, but all she really needed was a desk. Despite the small size, Jane liked it because it had an oval window beside the desk that looked out at the ocean. Jane didn't have time to look at the ocean, though. She was busy uploading the photos she'd taken of the guest rooms, the dining room, and the other parts of the inn that were in good repair, as well as the sandcastle cake, to the wedding venue website.

She hoped that the angle of a quaint oceanside inn offering lobster-bake weddings on the beach along with sandcastle wedding cakes would be enough to pique someone's interest.

Jane looked over the form, making sure everything

was correct. Was this the right thing to do? It was scary venturing into new territory, but what was the worst that could happen?

As she scoured the rest of the form, she noticed that the coastal wedding–listing website had a section for a link to her own website where the interested parties could reach her to ask for more info to book a wedding.

Darn it! She still had the old Tides website, and now she wanted to create a special section for weddings. Glancing at her email folder, she saw the third website developer had replied. Bad news. They were booked for a month.

She sighed, the old chair creaking as she leaned back. She looked out the window at the ocean. Now what was she going to do? She'd googled web designers in the area and come up empty. She supposed she didn't have to use someone local, though. Maybe she should expand her search.

A golden blur running on the beach caught her eye. Was that Cooper? She leaned forward, recognizing the tall figure of Mike as he threw a stick to the dog. The anxiety that had been roiling inside her eased. Just seeing the dog calmed her, as it probably did for many people. Maybe Claire was right and having a dog at the inn could be a benefit that would attract animal lovers.

But there wouldn't be any inn if she didn't get a

website designer. Wait a minute… hadn't Mike said that he was a freelance programmer? Programmers made websites, didn't they? Jane pushed up from the desk and hurried outside.

Cooper spotted Jane coming down the beach from two hundred yards away and made a beeline toward her, water flying off his fur as he ran. Jane crouched as the big dog practically bowled her over. She petted his wet and salty fur.

Beyond Cooper, Mike waved, jogging to catch up.

"Cooper sure has taken a liking to you," Mike said. "Fancy meeting you out here again."

Jane stood and looked down at Cooper, whose adoring brown eyes gazed back. "The feeling is mutual." Cooper nuzzled her hand, and she stroked his ears. "Actually, it's not a coincidence that I ran into you out here."

Mike's lips quirked in a grin. "Oh?"

His smile held a hint of flirtation that made butterflies swarm in Jane's stomach. This was crazy. She wasn't interested in Mike that way. She hadn't been interested in anyone that way since her husband and wasn't about to start now. "I was looking for you because I remembered you mentioned that you were a computer programmer."

"Yeah, that's what I do back in Seattle." Now Mike looked intrigued and maybe a bit confused.

"Well, it so happens that I need a website for Tides." Jane turned and pointed back toward the inn. "I was wondering if that's the sort of work you did, and if so, would you be looking for extra work while you're out here?"

"Yeah, I could do that. I'm pretty experienced with websites."

"Great." Jane kicked at a small white shell that had rolled up in the surf. Now for the hard part: the payment. Did freelance web designers charge a lot? Could Jane afford it? She didn't have much of a choice. If she didn't get the website in place, there would be no weddings booked, and not having an online booking system was a deterrent for guests who wanted to reserve a room online. "Great. What would you charge?"

Mike's gaze flicked to the inn, his expression uncertain, as if he could see how it needed repairs from here. "Charge? Well, to be honest, I'm not used to charging individual people. I usually work for companies, but I heard that Tides serves a hell of a good breakfast."

What did breakfast have to do with websites? "Yeah, we do."

"How about you just pay me with breakfast?" At Jane's skeptical look, he raised his hand. "No, no, I'm serious. I don't know how to cook, and I'm tired of cereal. You're not far down the beach, and I could get my morning walk in then stop for breakfast. That would be worth it for me."

"I hardly think a few breakfasts would pay your fee."

"You let me worry about that. Honestly, it's not a lot of work, and it would be more of a burden for me to have to come up with the invoices and so on for taxes. This would work out a lot better for me. When do you want to go over what you need?"

Somehow Mike made it sound like *she* was doing *him* a favor when she was sure it was the other way around. Jane couldn't afford to look a gift horse in the mouth. "I need something as soon as possible, so could we meet tomorrow? I'm busy in the morning, but I'll have our cook, Brenda, whip up something special for you, and maybe we could meet around eleven thirty?"

Mike rubbed his belly. "My mouth is watering already. Tomorrow it is."

"Great. See you then."

Jane stuck out her hand, and they shook to seal the

deal. She headed back to Tides, her heart a little lighter not only for seeing Cooper but for securing a great deal on getting the website done.

Mike watched Jane walk back to Tides, his hand still warm from their handshake. He was looking forward to the idea of working on the website, and not just because he'd get a hot breakfast. Spending more time with Jane definitely appealed to him. He didn't really need an extra job, but he could create websites in his sleep. She'd been right about the breakfasts not covering his fees—he charged a lot—but he didn't care about the money. He'd sensed that Tides wasn't doing that well and didn't want to take her money.

Cooper trotted along behind Jane.

"Cooper, back here!" Mike whistled for the dog, who stopped short, his attention wavering between Jane and Mike.

Jane turned and waved.

Mike picked up a stick and threw it, making the decision for the dog, who immediately raced in the direction of the stick.

Mike headed back toward his cottage throwing the stick, Cooper racing ahead then bringing it back. He was due to visit Gramps in an hour, and he wanted to go in and shower first. But Cooper needed to burn off some energy. Being cooped up in that small cottage all day wasn't good for him. He wouldn't be happy in Mike's apartment in Seattle, that was for sure.

"Mr. Henderson! Yoo-hoo!"

The woman Mike had rented his cottage from was standing on the deck waving him in. And not in a friendly nice-to-see-you way either. Judging by the rigid position of her body and the sour look on her face, she was not happy about something.

CHAPTER 11

*J*ane had been on pins and needles waiting for her sister to arrive.

She'd straightened the living room, dusted the foyer, and was now standing in the doorway picking away at the silver-foiled chocolate candy kisses that sat in the crystal ball on the table.

Her eyes drifted to the missing spindle on the stairs, the peeling paint on the old crown moldings, and the water stain in the upper corner on the wallpaper.

When had all this deterioration happened? Over the years, things had fallen into disrepair little by little, and she hadn't noticed. She didn't want Andie to think that she'd let the family business become run-down. Of course, it didn't help that Brenda had pointed out a bad

Yelp review stating the inn was in bad shape earlier that afternoon.

Think positive.

She had a lot to look forward to. Mike was going to work on the website, and she was sure he would get that done quickly. Chandler Vanbeck was checking in tomorrow, so at least they'd have two guests and the place wouldn't be totally empty.

Maxi was coming to help plan how to decorate for the weddings, and she'd submitted the application. Things were on an upswing.

Finally, a blue Volkswagen Jetta rental pulled up in front of the inn. Jane swiped at her mouth to remove any chocolate and smoothed her white linen shirt as she watched her sister get out of the car.

Strange feelings of warmth mixed with betrayal bubbled up. Jane could hardly blame her sister for leaving to pursue her dream career in New York, but she could've come back more frequently and at least shown a mild interest in the family business.

Still, her career must have agreed with her because Andie looked fabulous. She was wearing a sky-blue silk top over black capris with beaded black flip-flops on her feet. The sun hadn't quite set yet, and her large sunglasses and sleek dark hair that fell below her shoulders made her look like she should be featured in a magazine. Was her hair that color naturally? Jane touched her own pixie cut self-consciously. She'd let her hair go silver, but maybe she should have dyed it? She was the younger sister but felt like she looked like an old lady compared to Andie.

Jane took a deep breath and rushed outside to greet her sister.

Andie felt a surprising rush of emotion as she looked up at the big old house that had been so much a part of her life when she was younger. Even though she hadn't spent much time here in recent decades, it still felt familiar.

The old place was looking a little more dilapidated than when she'd seen it a year ago, but Andie didn't see any of that. All she saw was the porch she and her sister, Jane, had played on as kids, the garden her mother had lovingly tended, and the gorgeous cobalt-blue Atlantic Ocean beyond the building.

As she stepped out of the car, the salty sea smell hit her, and the sound of the waves calmed her. She immediately felt like a weight had been lifted. She was home.

Jane came rushing out of the front door. She looked good. She'd cut her hair, and it suited her. The casual shorts and linen shirt would make some people look dumpy, but not Jane. Jane looked classy.

Feelings of guilt replaced all those cozy feelings of home when she saw the look of strain on her sister's face. She should've been here to help more often.

They exchanged an awkward hug, and Andie resisted the urge to hold Jane close and apologize. Once, when they were younger, she would've known the right thing to say, but now she barely knew her little sister.

"Did you have a good flight?" Jane asked.

"Great. No turbulence." Andie popped open the trunk and hefted out her suitcase. "The place looks great."

Jane's forehead creased, and she turned to look at Tides. "Thanks."

Andie closed the trunk then stood there. "So, tell me the truth, sis. How is Mom?"

Jane shrugged. "She has her good days and her bad days. But she's getting very good care at Tall Pines. It's really the best place for her. I tried to keep her here at home as long as I could."

Andie felt terrible. Jane had struggled to keep their mom at home, and she could only imagine what that had been like. "It does sound like the best place. Are we going to see her tonight?"

Jane grabbed the suitcase and lugged it up the steps before Andie could stop her. "No, she has a routine over there. They eat dinner in twenty minutes, and then after that she's usually tired and goes to bed. I thought it was better not to disrupt that, so I figured we'd go early tomorrow morning." Jane turned to look at her. "I have some muffins and tea in the kitchen. I thought maybe you'd be hungry after traveling."

Andie smiled. She was starving. "That sounds great."

Andie followed Jane through the inn, taking note of the peeling paint and stained wallpaper. She didn't say a word, though. "How are things going here?"

"Great. I've got some ideas to bring in new business. You know, kind of modernize the place. Mom let things go a little bit, but I'm on top of it."

Andie sensed that her sister wasn't telling her the whole truth. She should've come back to help before this, but she'd been too wrapped up in her career and her stupid affair with Doug. Her sister had had a lot to handle here, but Jane had never let on how bad things had gotten. She'd never asked Andie for anything. Had she been such a bad sister over the years that Jane didn't even feel comfortable reaching out to her for help anymore?

"Sit down at the table and tell me how things are

going with you." Jane poured the tea into dainty cups that Andie remembered their grandmother serving them tea in. A plate with hand-painted forget-me-nots sat in the middle of the table, loaded with pastries. Andie chose an almond croissant.

"Things are going pretty much the same." Andie bit into the buttery, flaky croissant. "This is delicious."

"My friend Claire makes them at her bakery. You remember Claire, don't you?"

"Oh yeah, of course."

They chatted for an hour, getting caught up. Jane told her about helping their mom and how she was planning to host weddings and events to bring in more money. It sounded like Jane did have things under control, and that eased Andie's guilt a bit.

It was dark when Jane showed her to her room. It was the room she had slept in as a kid when they would stay here with their grandparents in the off-season, when the inn didn't have many guests. The floral wallpaper and creaky wooden floors brought a rush of cozy memories. The room was on the east side facing the ocean, and a bright crescent moon was high in the sky, sending golden light onto the flickering waves. She pulled out her phone expecting a text from Doug, but there was nothing.

Andie cracked the window open, letting in the scent

of the ocean and listening to the surf. She sat on the edge of the bed and took it all in, a peaceful feeling of calm coming over her. Should she be more upset that Doug had let her go without even saying goodbye and hadn't texted her? Maybe she wasn't as attached to him as she'd thought.

She put her clothes away and crawled between the crisp linen sheets that still smelled of Grandma's detergent. Much to her surprise, she immediately fell into a deep sleep.

CHAPTER 12

*E*arly the next morning, Jane drove Andie to Tall Pines. Somehow she thought the visit there would be less stressful with Andie at her side.

Don't get too used to it. Jane had no idea how long her sister would stay; they hadn't broached the subject the previous evening.

"This place is really nice." Andie surveyed the foyer with its muted soft-tone carpeting; soothing, slate-gray walls; and charming water fountain. "It must be expensive."

Jane paused. Was her sister going to complain about the cost? But when she looked at Andie, she only saw concern in her expression. "I'm hoping all the new things I have planned for Tides will cover Mom's care."

"Oh, good. I don't know much about the finances but wasn't sure. Didn't mean to pry."

"Don't worry. It's all being taken care of." Jane crossed her fingers even though it wasn't exactly a lie because she *was* trying to take care of it.

Laughter peeled out of Addie's room, and the two sisters exchanged a bemused glance. When they got to the doorway, they saw that Rob and Claire were there. Rob was kneeling down in front of Addie, flirting with her in that kind way he had. Naturally Addie was eating it all up.

"Andie, you remember my friend Claire, right?" Jane said gesturing toward Claire.

"Of course. How are you?" The two women shook hands, and then Jane introduced Andie to Rob, who stood to greet her.

"It's so nice of you guys to come and visit Mom," Jane said.

Claire gave her a hug. "Of course. She's like a second mother to me. Plus, I had some extra chocolate chip muffins."

"We'll let you visit with your mom alone." Rob took Claire's hand and led her from the room.

"Make sure you let Sadie Thompson know that Rob is my guy, and get back my sweater!" Addie yelled after them as they left.

Andie shot Jane a look of confusion. "Rob is her guy?"

Jane shrugged. "Sometimes Mom thinks so. We just let her think what she wants."

"Isn't Sadie Thompson the lady who has the big old house on the cliff? The oldest house in town?" Andie asked as she sat across from her mother and took her hand gently.

"Yep. She's an old friend of Mom's from when they were teens, remember?" Jane frowned. "I think they had some kind of falling out, but maybe not. Mom's memory about recent events isn't so great, but she remembers everything about when she was young."

"What's this about a stolen sweater, Mom?" Andie asked.

"Sweater?" Addie looked at Andie, her expression clouded, as if she didn't recognize her or remember about the sweater. Then suddenly her expression cleared, and she reached out to touch her arm. "Andie, you came. It's so nice of you."

Jane's heart almost broke seeing the looks on her sister's and mother's faces. She was glad her sister had come out. Obviously it was doing Addie good.

"Of course I came, Mom. Your room is great. Looks just like you wanted at Tides."

"I do love it here at Tides," Addie said.

Andie glanced at Jane. "It's a great place." Apparently, she agreed with just playing along.

"I'm going to go talk to the staff about some stuff and let you visit with Mom, okay?" Jane said.

Andie nodded and turned back to her mother. "Now, why don't you tell me about the sweater?"

Andie was glad her mother was in a nice place, but she'd changed so much since she'd last seen her that it was a bit of a shock. The last time she'd been out to visit her mother, she'd been forgetful, but not like this. As she held her mother's hand, she couldn't help but notice how fragile the tiny bones and paper-thin skin were.

"What sweater, Bridgie?" Addie used the nickname she'd called her older sister, Andie's Aunt Bridget. Bridget had died fifteen years ago, but Andie didn't correct her.

"You said you lost a sweater."

Addie nodded. "That's right. My sea-green sweater. I didn't lose it, though. That Sadie Thompson took it."

"She did? Huh, I'll have to see if I can get it back for you," Andie said, scanning the room for a green sweater lying about and coming up empty. Maybe it was in the bureau or closet. She'd look later. Right now it felt good just to sit here and hold her mother's hand.

Jane had done a good job. The room resembled their mother's bedroom at Tall Pines but with a few modern updates. And the place was nice. Andie couldn't have picked anything better herself. How was Jane paying for this? Hopefully she wasn't using her own retirement savings.

Judging by the state of things at Tides, there wasn't much money in the business. Her earlier comment about Tall Pines being expensive had raised her sister's hackles, indicating that broaching the subject of how it was being financed wasn't going to be easy. Andie would have to tread carefully on that, but if her sister needed financial help, she wanted to chip in. Not that she had a lot of money, but she could cut a bit here and save a bit there and maybe even dip into her own retirement savings.

"It was so good of you to come, dear," Addie said, pulling Andie from her thoughts. Now her mother's eyes were clear, and her smile had that sparkle Andie remembered. "How are things in New York?"

Suddenly her mother remembered who she was. Jane had said she had moments of clarity and moments of confusion. Andie would take the clarity when she could get it.

"Things are really good. I do love my job, and I've made a good life there." Except for Doug. Her mother didn't need to know about that, though. Getting involved with him had been a mistake, and one of the benefits of living away from home was that all your mistakes weren't flaunted in front of the whole town.

Addie scowled. "Well, I suppose the bright lights in the big city are fine for a while, but I don't think you've really made a life there. The city won't give you what you really want. Your roots are here."

Andie was shocked into silence. Her mother's memory might be failing, but her perception skills were spot on.

"Now, don't you forget about Tides. It's as much as part of the family as you and your sister are, and it needs to be kept up." Addie clutched Andie's hand with a surprisingly strong grip. "Promise to help your sister with the inn."

Andie covered her mother's hand with her other hand. "I promise, Mom."

"That's good, Bridget. I knew I could always count on you." Her mother's eyes turned cloudy again, her gaze drifting to the window. Andie's heart pinched. Her mother had gone back to the past. Maybe her mother thought that it was Bridgett who had just promised to help with the inn. That might be just as well, as Andie wasn't sure she could keep that promise, even if Jane wanted her to.

"Well, I guess Mom was right about one thing." Jane appeared in the doorway holding a sea-green sweater with seashell-shaped buttons down the front. "Sadie Thompson actually is here, and she really did have Mom's sweater."

CHAPTER 13

*M*axi took the scenic route to Tides, walking along the path on the ocean cliffs called the Marginal Way and then down across the beach once that path ended. She arrived right at ten, just as Jane had requested.

Jane was standing on the back deck, and a striking woman with long dark hair pulled up in a ponytail stood beside her. Was that Andie? Maxi hadn't seen her in years, since her visits to Lobster Bay were so infrequent.

"Andie, do you remember my friend Maxi?" Jane asked.

"Of course." Andie shook Maxi's hand. "How are you doing?"

"Fabulous. How are things in New York?"

Andie gave a half shrug, and Maxi sensed that maybe New York wasn't all she had hoped it would be. "It's okay. Right now I'm enjoying this amazing beach. You don't get that in the city. In fact, I was going to go take a walk on the beach. Unless you guys need me?" She looked at Jane.

"No, go ahead. Maxi and I are just going to discuss how we might decorate for a wedding here."

Andie hesitated for a second but then started down the steps onto the beach. "Okay, I'll leave you to it, then."

"How are things going with your sister?" Maxi asked as they watched her walk toward the surf.

"It's nice having her here, but I doubt she'll stay long, so there's no sense in having her in on any of these plans." Jane's voice didn't hold much emotion, but Maxi sensed regret and wondered if Jane wanted her sister to stay. It might be good for her if she did. Jane needed someone to be close to, especially now that her mother was at Tall Pines.

The back porch at Tides was wide, with an unobstructed view of the ocean. Living right on the ocean must be amazing. Sure, her house up on the cliff was nice, and it had a fabulous view, but to be down here right on the sand, listening to the waves crash on the beach and smelling the salty air, was a whole different experience.

"I was thinking the dance floor could go over there." Jane pointed to an area to the left of the house near the old garden. The garden used to be Jane's mother's pride and joy. She'd had a knack for gardening, and the whole area would be bursting with color and lush with greenery. Now it was overgrown and dotted with dead, dry leaves.

"Of course, I have to spruce up the gardens," Jane said, as if reading Maxi's mind.

They descended the steps, walking out onto the sand then turning to look back at the house.

"The tent would go over the dance floor, and the seating could be up on the deck for small weddings and then maybe under the tent for larger ones," Jane said. "That's what I know so far. Do you have any ideas as to how to make it cozy and unique?"

Maxi liked the idea of seating on the deck. It was under cover, so there would be good protection if it rained. She was brimming with ideas on how to make it unique. "How about getting some sheer drapes and hanging them at the corners of the deck and the sides of the tent? Bunch them up so they don't obstruct the view, but let them flutter in the breeze. It would add a dreamy feel to the wedding, and if you got the right type of rings, you could remove them when the wedding was over."

"That sounds perfect. I never would've thought of that!" Jane's eyes shone with an excitement that Maxi hadn't seen in a long time.

"And you need fairy lights. Depending on how you do the garden, we could twine them around some of the shrubs and string them on the tent. The deck, too, but we don't want to go overboard. You could keep the ones on the deck even when there isn't a wedding. And maybe add some lanterns with soft lights."

Jane clapped her hands together. "Another great idea. It would be magical."

"Yes." Maxi spun around, looking at the area, trying to picture it decked out for a wedding, searching for what else she might want to add. She pointed toward the ocean. "An arched arbor with roses climbing at the edge of the garden would be a perfect frame for the bride and groom to say their vows." She turned back to the house, pointing to the steps and running an imaginary trail with her finger. "You could roll out a runner on here for the bride to walk down the steps to the arbor."

"This all sounds amazing." Jane was thumbing notes into her phone. Maxi smiled. It felt good to be doing something productive and useful.

While Jane made notes, Maxi gazed out at the waves. The tide was coming in, so they were large, peaking up about three feet and then crashing into the beach. Farther to the right, where the tidal river met the open ocean, several surfers were bobbing in the water with surfboards, waiting to catch the perfect wave. Down near the edge of the water, a small dog chased a Frisbee, leaping into the air to catch it.

"That dog looks like he's having fun. Have you seen that one that you met at Tall Pines again?"

Jane looked up from her notes. "Yes, a few times. Actually, his owner, Mike, is doing my website."

"He is? How did that come about?" Maxi was intrigued. Jane wasn't the type to just ask strangers to work for her. She must really have taken a liking to the owner, as well as the dog.

Jane sighed. "Well, none of the contacts Claire gave me could do it in time, and I was having a hard time finding anyone else. He'd said he was a freelance programmer, so I figured I'd see if he needed extra work. He can do it right away, and I'm desperate."

"Oh, great. Is he expensive?"

"That's the best part. He'd heard about the breakfasts at Tides, and that's what he wants for payment."

Maxi's left brow quirked up. "Breakfast?"

"Yeah, I know it doesn't even out. I'll give him

money, too, but the point is it's not going to break my budget, and I'll get a website fairly quickly. We need it for the weddings, and Tammi said people want to book online these days. Plus, I get to see Cooper more. Actually, they're coming this morning to discuss what I want."

"That sounds perfect." Maxi tried not to smirk. She guessed Mike's interest might be in more than work but kept it to herself, as Jane appeared to be oblivious.

"Let's hope." Jane tapped her phone. "Thanks for these ideas. I really appreciate it."

"No problem. I'm happy to help. When you do book a wedding, just let me know, and I'll come over and make some of these ideas come to life for real."

They hugged, and Maxi headed back down the beach. She hoped that Jane would get the wedding and be able to start making Tides profitable again. And she couldn't wait to meet this mysterious Mike and his dog. She had a feeling things were about to get interesting.

CHAPTER 14

*J*ane sat at the old table in the kitchen, her laptop open and her attention wavering from the screen showing her bank account balance to the whopping electric bill in her hand. The air-conditioning at Tides cost a small fortune. The inn had been built before central air-conditioning was invented, and they didn't have a complete house-wide system. She relied on window air conditioners and a few wall units her father had had put in years ago. Good thing she had Sally working on the weatherproofing. That would cut down future costs, but that wasn't going to help her with *this* bill.

Eventually she'd modernize the air-conditioning and heating systems, but right now she couldn't afford that. Nor could she afford this electric bill. The utility budget for the year had already been spent, and it was only July. How long could she go before they shut it off? She certainly couldn't risk that, and the bill was due tomorrow. She'd have to divert some funds from the account she used to pay the food-supply company that delivered to the inn.

The food bill wasn't due for another two weeks. Hopefully money would come in between now and then to pay it. As an accountant, Jane knew that taking all the money from one account to pay another was not a healthy way to run a business, but what choice did she have?

"Thank God, coffee's brewing." Andie came into the kitchen, and Jane folded the utility bill back up and slipped it into the envelope. Andie didn't need to worry about the inn's financial troubles.

Andie poured coffee into a white ceramic mug and leaned against the counter, sipping. "I was out walking the beach. What are you doing?"

"Just tending to some of the finances of the inn." Jane closed the laptop and smiled at her sister.

"Running the inn is a lot to handle. I really appreciate that you do this," Andie said.

Jane was taken aback by her sister's kind words. Was it wrong not to tell Andie about the financial troubles? But what good would it do to tell her? She would be leaving, and everything would be up to Jane. No sense in even talking about it.

"I've spent a lot of the past year taking care of Mom, and some things are falling by the wayside. But now that Mom is safe at Tall Pines, I'm going to fast-track repairs and get this place up to full earning potential. Of course, I have Sally, but I've also hired someone else to help out.

"In fact, I think you know the person. It's Shane Flannery," Jane said. "That's the guy you used to date, right?"

Andie shrugged, staring into her coffee. "Yeah, just a bit."

Just a bit? Jane seemed to remember that they were inseparable, if Shane Flannery was the one she was thinking of. So many years had gone by. Her memory was actually a little shaky, and at the time, she'd been sixteen and too self-involved to worry too much about her sister's love life.

But judging by the way Andie wouldn't make eye contact and seemed a bit *too* disinterested, she had the distinct feeling her sister's relationship with Shane Flannery had been more than her sister was letting on.

"When is he coming?" Andie turned to top off her mug.

"Later this afternoon." Jane watched her sister,

amused.

"Oh." Andie fell silent, working on her coffee for a few sips. "Do you need any help with anything around here?"

"No. You're on vacation, you should enjoy yourself. Go out on the beach," Jane said, even though she actually could use help. A *lot* of help.

She didn't want her sister to know that, though. If Andie kept the same pattern she had before, she wouldn't be staying long, so there was no sense in getting her involved in a project.

Jane glanced at the clock over the stove. It was almost eleven thirty, and Mike would be here soon to talk about the website. Would he bring Cooper? Jane hoped so.

Andie stood at the edge of the surf, her coffee mug in her hand, tentatively dunking a toe in the water. She'd forgotten how frigid the ocean could be in Maine, even in the middle of summer.

She turned and looked back at Tides. It was still a magnificent house, even if it did need a few repairs. A surge of love for the inn bubbled up. She wanted Tides to succeed, but she was worried because it needed a lot of care. Jane had said she didn't need help, but was that just her pride talking?

Andie had made a promise to her mother about helping Jane. Even though her sister pushed her off, she wanted to do *something* useful while she was here. As a girl, she'd loved working in the garden with her mom. Maybe that was something she could do to help out.

She headed toward the garden, slipping her phone out of her pocket to check for messages. Still no text from Doug, but that didn't bother her. She'd almost forgotten to even look. It was as if being at the ocean had a cleansing effect where he was concerned.

The garden needed some serious tending. The weeds had taken over most of the flowerbeds, but Andie could still see purple cone flowers, brilliant red monarda, and clumps of black-eyed Susans. It would take some weeding, some bark mulch, and a few new flowers here and there, but these beds could be beautiful again.

Her mother had always planted impatiens and pansies along the garden edge. Andie had usually helped with that task, under her mother's instruction. Now she'd have a chance to see if she'd inherited her mother's green thumb.

Her mother had always put out bird feeders too. Some of Andie's fondest memories were sitting and watching the jewel-toned hummingbirds battle around the feeders. No feeders were out in the garden now, but did they even still have them?

On the other side of the driveway that circled around the front of the house sat the three- car garage attached to the old outhouse the family used for storage. Her grandfather had called the outhouse a three-seater. His stories of how he and his two brothers would use it at the same time for warmth in the frigid winters had always had Andie and Jane giggling. By the time Andie and Jane had come along, indoor plumbing had been installed, but the structure still stood. It was useful for storage, though it did need a good paint job.

She rummaged around inside, pushing spiderwebs and dust away until she found the familiar red-topped glass hummingbird feeder. It was a little dusty but in good condition, with little perches shaped like flowers on the bottom.

She'd forgotten how fun it was to watch the tiny birds. They didn't have any of those in New York City —or if they did, she'd never seen one. Maybe she'd been too busy working to take the time?

If memory served correctly, all she had to do was mix one part sugar to four parts water to make the nectar. She headed back to the house, eager to get the bird feeder set up as soon as possible.

CHAPTER 15

*J*ane was just finishing up with the accounting when Mike appeared at the kitchen door. Much to her delight, Cooper was at his side.

"Thanks for coming." Jane bent down to pet the dog. "Brenda made a breakfast plate for you. Why don't you get settled at the table, and I'll heat it up."

Mike took his laptop out of the bag and sat at the table while Jane heated up the plate of eggs, sausage, and pancakes that Brenda had set aside.

"So, what exactly do you want in a website?" Mike asked as he shoveled in the breakfast. "This is delicious, by the way."

"Darn tootin'. Brenda makes the best breakfast,"

Sally piped in without even taking her eyes off her current job of fixing the hinges on one of the corner cabinets.

"Can't argue with that." Jane slid her laptop around so Mike could see the screen. "I surfed around the internet and found some examples of what I would like our website to look like. Of course, I'll need a form that people can fill out with information on weddings. And also, it needs to be hooked up to some sort of a reservation system—even if it just sent me an email—as long as the people can fill the form out online."

Mike studied the example sites she had on her screen. "Looks simple enough. Should be easy." He shoved his plate aside and started typing notes on his own laptop. "I should have a mock-up ready for you tomorrow. Is that okay?"

"So soon? That would be great. You don't need to rush on my account, though."

"I'm not rushing. I'll put together some examples. Then we can go through it, and you can tell me what needs to be changed."

"I really appreciate this," Jane said as Mike started packing up his laptop. "Are you sure you don't want payment? I know website designers cost a lot."

Mike smiled and shook his head. "No. Seriously, the breakfast is enough."

"We'll be sure to have a good one ready for you when you come tomorrow." Jane knelt down in front of Cooper, running her fingers through his thick fur. "And I guess I'll see you tomorrow too."

"Actually, you might not." Mike's voice sounded grim. Jane glanced up at him, and his expression indicated that something was wrong.

"What do you mean?" Jane asked.

Mike sighed. "The landlady that I'm renting the cottage from said I can't have pets. Even though on the Airbnb listing, it did say pets were allowed, now she's saying that was a mistake, and I can't keep Cooper there. No place else is available in town, so I'm going to have to put him in the kennel until I figure out something permanent."

"A kennel?" Jane's heart pinched at the trusting look in Cooper's whiskey-brown eyes. He seemed so happy, wagging his tail, eagerly awaiting another walk on the beach. Images of the dog sad and depressed and crammed into a dirty kennel with no beach to run on came to mind. "Surely there's got to be something else you can do?"

"I wish there was. I'm not putting him up for adoption or anything yet, but I'll have to keep him somewhere and come and take him out to visit Gramps."

"But he'll be in a small kennel all day. That won't

do. What if he stayed here instead?" Jane had blurted the proposition out before she knew it was coming, but now that it was out, she didn't regret it. Having Cooper at Tides felt right.

Mike's eyes widened. "Oh, I couldn't ask you to do that."

"Of course you can. You can consider it partial payment for the website. You'd have to pay a lot to have Cooper stay in a kennel, right?"

Mike's gaze flicked from Jane to Cooper. "I don't know. It seems like an imposition."

Jane stepped over to Cooper and patted his head. "No imposition at all. In fact, it will be a joy to have him here."

Mike still looked uncertain, but Jane could see that he liked the idea of having Cooper at Tides a lot more than putting him in a kennel. Who wouldn't?

"Okay. Well, if you put it that way, I guess I can't refuse."

"It's a deal, then." Jane stuck out her hand, and they shook. Letting the handshake linger a little bit longer than necessary, she looked up. Their eyes met.

"Ahem!"

Jane dropped Mike's hand and looked over to see Andie standing in the doorway.

"Oh, Andie. This is Mike Henderson. He's making the website for Tides. Mike, my sister, Andie."

The two of them shook hands, and Jane thought she saw an amused smirk on her sister's face. Why would her sister be amused at Mike making a website?

Jane gestured toward the dog. "And this is Cooper. He's going to be staying here."

Andie's brows shot up. "Oh? That's great. I love dogs."

Andie held up an old glass hummingbird feeder. "I was just coming to make some nectar for the hummingbird feeder. I thought I might spruce up the gardens."

"That's a great idea. They could use it." Apparently, Andie wasn't rushing back to New York. Sprucing up the gardens would take a few days at least. Jane felt cautiously encouraged about her sister's involvement in Tides.

"Okay. Well, I guess I'll see you tomorrow morning, then. I'll show you the website example and collect Cooper to go visit Gramps." Mike nodded at both the girls and left through the back door.

Andie tried to keep the smirk off her face as she

watched Mike leave. She and Jane hadn't been that close in recent years, but she was pretty sure her sister hadn't even thought about dating since Brad died. But the attraction between Jane and Mike was obvious. At least it was to Andie. Jane, on the other hand, seemed oblivious. Mike, not so much. Well, good for them. Just because Andie wasn't doing well in the relationship department didn't mean she wasn't happy for others who were. Besides, Mike seemed nice, and he was kind of cute.

She pulled the jar of sugar out of the cabinet and started measuring for the nectar. "So, you're revamping the website?"

"Bringing it up to more modern times," Jane said. "The old website is so outdated. People want to be able to book rooms online these days. Plus, if we have weddings, we need information about them on the site and a form for people to fill out online."

Andie squatted down so her eyes were at counter level, making sure she'd put the right amount of sugar in the measuring cup. "That sounds like a smart idea."

Woof!

Cooper was standing at the door, staring down the beach after Mike. He wagged his tail, looking from Jane to the door.

"Sorry, buddy, you're going to be staying here. You'll see Mike later." Jane patted her leg, and the dog cast one last look out the door then sat beside her, staring up at Jane adoringly.

"I think he's getting attached to you." Andie thought Jane might be getting attached too.

"He's a good boy." Jane massaged his neck. "Oh darn. We're going to need dog food and bowls and supplies."

"I think I saw some bowls when I was looking for the bird feeder in storage," Andie said. "I can grab those and pick up some other supplies on the way home from visiting Mom at Tall Pines." Andie leaned against the counter and looked at her sister slyly. "Unless you want an excuse to call Mike."

Jane looked genuinely confused. "Of course I don't want an excuse to call him. Why would I?"

Andie gave her a look, and Jane blushed.

"That's silly. He's just making my website, and besides, he's too young for me." Jane glanced out the door, where they could still see Mike walking down the beach.

"He's not that young. I know his family," Sally piped in from where she was still working on the hinge. "Aren't you about forty-eight?"

"Yes," Jane said.

Sally looked up at the ceiling as she did mental calculations. "Let's see now. Mike was born the year that Jesse had Brady, so that makes him... yep, he's forty-one. That's only seven years."

"That seems like a big difference to me," Jane said.

"Not really. Mom was ten years older than Dad," Andie said.

Jane scoffed. "I'm not in the market for a boyfriend."

Jane sounded like she was protesting a little bit too much, but Andie decided to let it go. She glanced over at Sally. Judging by the look on Sally's face, she agreed.

Sally shoved her screwdriver into one of the slots in her toolset and then bent to pet Cooper. "I think Cooper will be a good addition here. Are you ready to discuss some of the ongoing work? Shane is going to be here in a few minutes."

The mention of Shane's name jolted Andie into action. She did not want to be here when Shane arrived. She felt guilty for the way she'd treated him and didn't know what to say to him. Should she apologize? Or had so much time gone by that it was no longer an issue? Better to not run into him at all.

"Gotta run! I'm going to go visit Mom at Tall

Pines." She quickly poured the nectar in the feeder and headed to the garden.

Out in the lobby, a man was standing at the check-in desk. She hesitated. Should she check him in? She didn't know the first thing about the process, but it seemed rude to just walk past him.

"Andie?" The man turned, and she recognized him as Chandler Vanbeck.

"Chandler? What are you doing here?"

"I'm thinking of opening an art gallery in town. I've never stayed at this inn before, but the location is great, so I figured I'd try it." He looked up at the ceiling, the wallpaper, and the broken spindles on the stairs. "It's quaint. Are you staying here too?"

"I suppose you could say that. This is my family's inn. But I am just visiting on vacation." Andie glanced out nervously at the driveway. Shane would be here any minute. She didn't want to be hanging out in the lobby like a sitting duck when he arrived.

"Oh, that's great. Nice place. I didn't realize you were from back East."

Jane, Sally, and Cooper came out into the lobby. Chandler's eyes lit up when he saw the dog. "You have a resident dog? Delightful. Now I know I made the right decision."

Andie took the opportunity to make her exit. "I

guess I'll let you get checked in. I'll see you later." She hurried outside, the nectar sloshing around in the feeder and spilling out some of the holes, but she didn't care. She was in a hurry to get it set up in the garden and get the heck out of there.

CHAPTER 16

Shane Flannery arrived exactly when he was supposed to. Jane had heard stories about contractors habitually being late, so this set things off on the right foot. Hopefully Shane would continue to be prompt. Sally introduced them, and Shane shook her hand.

"Jane. How are you? It's been a while." He had an easy, friendly way about him, and Jane liked him immediately.

The gangly teenager who had dated Andie had grown into an attractive man. Years in the navy had broadened his shoulders. He stood straight, with cropped dark hair graying at the temples and kind gray eyes with crinkles at the edges. Jane wondered what Andie would think when she saw how he'd turned out.

Shane didn't ask about Andie, but his eyes kept drifting over Jane's shoulder, as if he were looking for someone. Maybe he was just scoping the place out to see what he was getting himself into.

"We have a lot of projects going on here," Sally said. "As you can see, there's a lot of cosmetic repairs, but we have some other things going on too. Let's walk through, and I'll go over everything with you."

Jane let Sally take over. She knew more of the specifics of the work that needed to be done, and she and Shane spoke the same language. Shane offered some good suggestions on some of the projects, and Jane could tell that he and Sally would work well together. He knew his stuff too. Before they were even halfway through the tour, Jane had already decided that she wanted to hire him.

Cooper stuck by her side the whole time they were walking through the house. It felt good to have him there. And every time she looked down, he would glance up with that adoring look in his eye.

She was taking a risk. Having a dog at the inn might turn off some potential guests, but if Chandler Vanbeck's reaction was any indication, it might also attract others. And besides, there was no way she was going to let Cooper go to the kennel now.

Sally ended the tour outside in the spot where

they'd decided to put the temporary dance floor should someone book a wedding.

"You think we can build something that will withstand a lot of dancing and still be able to be taken apart and stored away in the outbuildings?" Sally asked Shane.

Shane dug the toe of his boot into the sand. "It's pretty soft, but I've built something similar. We may need to tamp down the area, but it shouldn't be a problem."

"Good, because I think having weddings is going to be a really good business venture for Tides." Sally glanced over at Jane. "Shane's divorced, you know."

Shane laughed at Sally's blunt words. "Well, that was a long time ago. I don't think working on additions for weddings is going to bother me."

"He's got a cute grandson now, though," Sally added.

Shane beamed.

Sally looked at Shane and cocked her head to the side. "Say, didn't you used to date Jane's sister, Andie?"

Shane shifted on his feet, looking embarrassed to be put on the spot. "A little bit. That was a long time ago."

"She's still single," Sally blurted out.

Jane and Shane both looked at Sally, and she put her hand over her mouth.

"Was that inappropriate? Sorry, I'll mind my own business from now on."

Shane simply shook his head and laughed. "Now come on, Sally, you know minding your own business is impossible for you."

Sally did not look the least bit contrite. She often meddled, but she had good intentions.

"Andie's actually in town now. She's visiting our mom at Tall Pines, but I suppose it won't be long until the two of you run into each other here at Tides," Jane said.

"Oh, good." Shane's tone was flat.

Jane couldn't tell if Shane looked hopeful or terrified, but either way it would prove to make things interesting in the days to come.

Andie returned from Tall Pines with bags of supplies for Cooper. Jane made tea, and they settled on the soft, comfortable couches in the living room. This room had tall windows that overlooked the ocean, and it was Jane's favorite. Cooper flopped down on the floor in-between them. None of the guests were around, so they had the room to themselves.

"I wasn't sure what kind of food Cooper ate, so I

got a few different brands." Andie pulled several bags of dog food out of the shopping bag.

"Brenda was worried he might be hungry. She made him boiled chicken and rice, so he probably won't even eat commercial dog food anymore," Jane joked, looking down at Cooper, who thumped his tail on the floor.

Andie bent down and addressed the dog while running her hand along his back. "Well, I guess we don't have to worry about you going hungry."

"How was Mom?" Jane looked into one of the bags. It held a variety of dog toys. Plush animals, rubber toys, a rope.

"She was fine, but I had a little scare when I got there. She wasn't in her room," Andie said.

Jane looked up from inspecting the bag, worry blooming in her chest. Had Addie started wandering away from her room? "She wasn't?"

"No. She was in the craft room working on a puzzle. One of the nurses said it was a good sign that she wasn't just sitting in her room alone. She's getting involved in doing things. She seemed really happy," Andie said.

Jane supposed that was a good sign. She had expected it to take longer for her mother to acclimate to her new environment, but this was better. She was glad her mom was settling in and happy, but it made the responsibility of having to make Tides a success weigh on her even more heavily.

"I noticed the hummingbirds have come to the feeder you put in the garden. Do you have plans for sprucing it up?" Jane asked. Seeing the jewel-toned birds buzz around the feeder had brought back memories of when they were kids. Jane felt bad that she hadn't been able to keep up with it, but she'd been so busy this last year with running the inn and taking care of their mother that there had been no time. Gardens took a fair bit of time to maintain, which made Jane wonder what Andie was planning. If she was going to rush back to New York City, she didn't want her digging up the garden and making a mess that she couldn't finish.

"Remember how Mom used to plant those white-and-pink striped impatiens all along the border and then have those hostas in the middle?" Andie's face lit up as she talked about the garden. She always had been more interested in gardening than Jane. "I checked at the gardening store, and those plants aren't that expensive. I think I'd like to put those in just like Mom did. And, of course, I'll weed and get some new mulch. You have a lot of repairs here at Tides, and I know there might not be anything in the budget for all that, so I'll just pay for it myself."

"You don't have to do that. Just give me the receipt. It's a tax write-off." Jane paused then glanced over at her sister. "So, you're staying a while, then?"

Andie sat back in the chair and sighed. "Maybe." She looked down at her feet. "Work isn't going that great."

Jane felt a pang of sympathy. "I'm sorry to hear that. There's plenty for you to do here, so if you need to take a break from your job, I can keep you busy."

Footsteps in the hallway interrupted their conversation.

Chandler Vanbeck appeared in the doorway. He looked at them uncertainly. "Am I interrupting?"

"'Course not, come in," Jane said. The living room and common areas were always open for guests. Her great-grandparents had wanted the inn to be like a home away from home and provide a comfortable family setting, and Jane intended to continue that.

Chandler came into the room, and Cooper immediately walked over to greet him with a friendly sniff. Chandler smiled and petted the dog. "This place is lovely. I was out on the beach earlier, and it's an amazing spot. Andie, you never mentioned your family had such a great property."

Andie gazed out at the ocean. "I know. I guess it never came up."

Chandler had wandered over to the east wall and was eyeing the collage of gilt-framed paintings. The paintings dated back to Jane's great-grandparents' time. Old landscapes, vibrant ocean scenes.

"You have quite the collection here. Some of these paintings are quite valuable." Chandler turned to look at them. "You wouldn't be interested in selling any of them, would you?"

Jane was startled by the thought. The paintings had been there since before she was born.

"These paintings have been in our family forever. We would never sell them." She turned to her sister. "Would we?"

Andie shook her head. "No, they're like family heirlooms. We couldn't part with them."

Chandler smiled sheepishly. "Oh well. I hope I didn't offend you. It's just that one can't help but be interested when you run into something exquisite in my line of work. You know how it is, Andrea."

Andie nodded. "We're not offended, are we, Jane?"

Jane shook her head. "Of course not."

The inn was filled with antiques, paintings, furniture, and knickknacks. The thought of selling them had never crossed Jane's mind. She could practically feel her ancestors looking down and shaking their heads. She couldn't possibly part with anything in the inn...

not unless she was absolutely desperate. Thankfully, she hadn't gotten to that point yet. All she needed was to ramp up the bookings, book a wedding, or come up with an idea for some other type of event.

Chandler headed to his room, and Jane and Andie chatted for a bit longer before taking Cooper out to do his business and then heading to bed. Jane was surprised at how Cooper took to living at the inn. He simply followed her up to her room and lay down.

Jane fell asleep, feeling more hopeful than she had been in weeks.

CHAPTER 17

*J*ane's bedroom faced east, and she was used to the rising sun peeking in at an early hour. What she wasn't used to was the warm body in bed beside her. She startled awake when a wet nose against her hand reminded her about Cooper. He'd started off on the floor but must have made his way into the bed during the night. Jane didn't mind.

"Come on, boy. You probably have to go out, right?" Jane wasn't used to having another being to consider, but she was happy to make the adjustment. She took Cooper outside to do his business and then fed him before even getting a cup of coffee for herself.

Settled at the kitchen table with an English muffin

on her plate and Brenda cooking in the background, Jane checked her email and practically fell off her chair.

Brenda turned around, concerned. "Is something wrong, Jane?"

"Someone wants to book a wedding."

"Really? That's good isn't it?" Brenda asked.

"Of course. It's just a surprise. I wasn't expecting something this quick, and they want it in less than five weeks." Jane started to panic. How was she going to pull together a wedding in a month? She didn't know anything about weddings. Why had she signed up for this?

Brenda, unflappable as usual, forked the bacon out of the pan, laying it on paper towels. "Nothing wrong with getting more money sooner."

Brenda had a point. She'd just taken money allotted for the food service to pay the electric bill. If she could pull this wedding off, she'd get a deposit and should be able to replace that money without having to be overdue on the bill to the food supplier.

She read the comments on the form application carefully. "It's a rush job because the place they had booked closed down without notice. It's for fifty people, and they're excited about a beach wedding and lobster bake. Do you think we can handle that?"

"Of course we can. And just think, maybe they'll

book all the rooms." Brenda seemed happy at the prospect of being able to cook breakfast for a full house.

The applicant wanted pictures of the actual outdoor area where the wedding would be and a description of Jane's plan. Plan? Was she supposed to have a plan? She'd be filling the role of wedding planner, but how hard could a small beach wedding be to plan?

The comments on the form specified that they wanted something classy, not a venue with picnic tables and porta potties. If they liked what Jane sent and her quote was reasonable, they would send a twenty-five percent deposit right away.

Jane's mind whirled as she thought about what she should send them for a plan. She wanted more pictures. Maybe some close-ups of the work Andie was doing on the garden and one of the ocean framed by the arbor. She already had basics of the rooms and interior of Tides up on the website, but she didn't have any of how it would look at an actual wedding. Maybe Maxi could help with that.

Mike was due any minute to go over the website, and Jane wanted to visit her Mom at Tall Pines, so she asked Maxi to come later that afternoon.

There! She'd put the plans in motion. This could really work.

Cooper let out a sudden woof and rushed to the screen door. Jane looked up to see Mike, his laptop bag slung over his shoulder.

Cooper's exuberant greeting lightened Mike's heart. The night in the cottage without the dog had been lonely. Cooper wagged his tail and wiggled as Mike crouched down and hugged him.

"I missed you, big guy." He was getting attached. Not only to Cooper but to the ocean, to the town, to the people.

"I think he might've missed you, too, at least for a little bit, until Brenda made him chicken and rice," Jane teased.

"Ha ha. Seriously, how did he do? I hope he was no trouble." Mike wrestled the laptop out of his bag and put it on the table.

"Not at all. He adjusted quite well, and I love having him," Jane said.

"He's a good boy." Brenda tossed Cooper a small piece of bacon and slid a plate in front of Mike. It was overflowing with scrambled eggs, bacon, hash browns, and toasted English muffins.

Mike dug in, looking up at Jane every few seconds.

She had a spark in her eye today, and her face was flushed. He suspected something exciting had happened but felt awkward asking. "I feel rude eating in front of you."

"I already ate. But I am eager to see the website. I got a booking for a wedding, so things are starting to come together."

So *that* was why she looked so excited. His assumption about Tides doing poorly financially must have been true. A wedding would bring in a lot of money. "That's great! Tell me more."

"It's in a month, so I'm going to have to hustle. Apparently, the venue they had booked closed down suddenly." Jane blew out a breath. "I'm a little nervous about taking it on, but I think it will be good for Tides."

"What can I do to help?" Mike asked.

Jane looked surprised, like she hadn't been expecting him to offer to help. "I guess just putting the website up would be a big help."

Mike set his plate aside. "Then I guess we should get started, and I'll show you what I've got."

He proceeded to show her several pages of the website that were similar to the examples she'd shown him but with pictures and text specific to Tides. The navigation still wasn't set up, since he wasn't sure if she'd want changes. Of course, he had the contact page, and he'd installed a form where one could book online and generate an email to Jane.

"You might want to consider integrating a calendar that will block off dates. Right now you'd have to go back and forth with email to confirm the booking," Mike said. "There might be a plug-in or program you can buy. I can look into that for you."

"That would be great. I love what you have so far," Jane said.

"Then I should go ahead and finish it up?"

"Yes."

"Okay. It won't take me long to get everything hooked up and working properly." Mike slung the laptop bag over his shoulder then hesitated. "I want to take Cooper to visit Gramps at Tall Pines today. Can I swing by later and get him?"

"Of course. Come by any time. No need to ask permission. We have people coming and going from here all the time. I was actually going to Tall Pines myself to visit my mom right after this." Jane looked at her watch, and Mike got the impression she might be in a hurry. He almost collided with Andie on his way to the door. She was holding the hummingbird feeder.

"Those birds sure drink a lot of nectar," Mike said.

Andie laughed. "They do, but this is actually a

second feeder. Hummingbirds are territorial and will fight, so we put feeders at either end of the garden."

"Who knew?" Mike said goodbye to Cooper while Andie filled the feeder in record time.

When she was done, she sidestepped the dog on her way to the pantry.

"Why are you going out that way?" Jane asked, looking confused. "Wouldn't it be shorter to go through the lobby?"

Andie stopped and looked at her sister. "Probably, but I don't want to spill nectar in there."

Jane glanced at Mike, her expression indicating she thought Andie wasn't making much sense. "Okay, whatever suits you."

But Andie had already headed off through the pantry, which, from what Mike knew of the layout, seemed to be a roundabout route.

Mike gave Cooper another pat on the head and set off down the beach. Maybe he would extend his stay in Lobster Bay. Gramps had perked up a lot since Mike had come to visit, and the scenery didn't hurt. Plus, he was making new friends... like Jane. Besides, he liked it here. Things were more laid-back, and he was getting attached to Cooper.

His phone dinged, and he pulled it out to see a text from Tiffany.

Wondering when you're coming back?

Mike rolled his eyes. Apparently, he'd need to have another talk with her. She certainly wasn't getting the hint. How could he possibly make it clearer that he didn't want to date her anymore? He'd told her so in no uncertain terms. She just wasn't getting the message. Maybe it was time he blocked her number.

Andie rushed through the pantry, away from Jane and her darn questions. The truth was that she was avoiding the lobby because she'd seen Shane in there earlier fixing the spindle on the staircase. It was silly because it had been decades since she'd broken up with him, but she just didn't want to talk to him. Why add more stress to her life? There was no point in reconnecting since she would be leaving Lobster Bay soon enough.

She turned left, intending to cut through the dining room and then go out the side door, except—

"Watch out! That paint is wet!"

Over thirty years had passed, but Andie recognized Shane Flannery in an instant. They stood staring at each other, and the years peeled away. It was as if they were both awkward high school seniors again. Except Shane

162

looked way better than he had back then. How unfair was that?

"Andie. Hi." Shane smiled, revealing the dimple on his right cheek.

"Hi." Andie's tongue appeared to be stuck to the roof of her mouth.

"How are you?"

"Good. You?" Andie tried to add something clever, but nothing came out.

"Pretty good. Got out of the navy, and now I do carpentry work." He gestured toward the room, where there was clearly a big project going on. "You're standing on Sally's brush."

"What?" Andie's gaze jerked down, and she lifted her right foot to reveal a squashed brush. The bottom of her flip-flop was smeared with red paint. "Crap!"

"Yeah, Sally's not going to be happy you ruined her brush."

Shane looked amused as Andie tried to balance removing the flip-flop with one hand while trying not to spill the nectar she was holding in her other. He could have offered to help!

"Well, nice seeing you." Shane turned back to his work, and Andie hobbled off.

Seriously, was that it? She didn't know what she had expected, but the interaction with Shane felt like a slight. She was probably being overly sensitive. It had been decades since they'd seen each other, so there was no reason to act like they were buddies. Even though they'd dated, that was so long ago. He'd been married since then, and of course he was over her. Probably barely even remembered they'd dated. And what did it matter? She'd gotten over him long ago. Hadn't she?

CHAPTER 18

*J*ane had a momentary surge of panic when she got to Tall Pines only to find that Addie wasn't in her room.

One of the nurses, Gloria, noticed her standing at Addie's door. "She's up in the art room."

"Art room?" Jane remembered taking the tour when she'd first looked at Tall Pines. They had several recreation rooms. She hadn't pictured her mother using any of them and hadn't paid much attention. She'd been more concerned about the rooms themselves, the meals, and, most importantly, the price.

Gloria nodded. "She's painting with another resident, Stella Ambrose."

"Really?" Her mother had made friends this quickly?

Gloria smiled. "Go see for yourself. It's on the second floor, end of the hall to the right."

The art room was large, with long tables and easels at the front. Light spilled in from a large palladium window. Addie was standing at one of the easels, her concentration focused on the work in front of her. A short woman with colorful glasses and short, spiked white hair dabbed large blobs of paint on the canvas at the easel next to her.

Neither woman had seen Jane come in, and she paused to watch her mother. Addie looked happy, serene. Other than keeping the gardens up, Addie had never had time for hobbies while running Tides. At least maybe her mother could get a chance to unleash her creativity during this stage of her life.

Jane entered the room and stood behind Addie. "That's beautiful, Mom."

The other woman turned to address her. "Thank you, dear!"

"Umm... you're welcome." Jane hadn't been talking to the woman or even looking at her work.

Addie laughed. "Now don't be silly, Stella. Jane is *my* daughter."

Jane was encouraged that her mother remembered her.

"Oh, sorry." Stella laughed. "You look a lot like my daughter."

At least Stella was taking it on the chin.

Addie dipped her paintbrush in a cup of white paint and motioned Jane closer. "Come over here, and I'll show you a little trick I learned."

The painting was really just a bunch of colorful splashes, sort of modernistic in a way. Jane wondered what Chandler Vanbeck would think of it.

Addie's demeanor was serious as she focused on the painting, placing the brush very carefully in the middle of the blue splotch and making a perfect white dot. "See? If you put a little white spot here, it makes it look like a reflection."

"I see. That's a great tip," Jane said.

"Yes, well." Addie stepped back, putting the paintbrush in a mason jar filled with water. "I think that's enough for today. I smell lunch, and I don't want to miss it because it's grilled cheese. Would you like to stay, Jane?"

Jane would've loved to have stayed now that it was one of her mother's lucid times, but she couldn't. She had to meet Maxi at Tides. She longed to tell her mother about the wedding and ask for her advice, but she was afraid it might confuse her, so instead she simply smiled and patted her mother's arm. "I have to run, but you have a good time at lunch. Do you need anything?"

Addie laughed and gestured around the room. "What would I possibly need? I have everything I could ever want right here."

Jane left tall Pines feeling like at least part of the weight on her shoulders had been lifted.

Maxi power walked along the beach, her footsteps leaving deep prints in the wet sand. She'd chosen to walk to Tides for her meeting with Jane, even though it was almost two miles from her house. She needed to clear her head after the disturbing discovery she'd made while cleaning out the pockets of James's suit before taking it to the dry cleaner.

Maybe it wasn't such a great idea to bring a heavy bag of sketching stuff, though, she thought as she hitched her blue-striped tote bag up onto her shoulder. But bringing along a sketch pad, pencils, and water-color pens was necessary if she wanted to paint after she left Tides.

The tide was out, so the shoreline where she was walking was almost the length of a football field away from the buildings. Glancing over, she could see the big white structure of Tides. Jane was standing on the porch.

Maxi took a deep breath of calming ocean air, let it out slowly, then headed up on the dry sand to meet Jane. Plastering on a smile, she waved as she approached the inn.

"You walked?" Jane asked.

"Yep. Need my exercise." Maxi made power-walking motions. A golden retriever trotted over from where he'd been sniffing the rosebushes. Maxi's spirits lifted. Animals always made her feel better. "Is this Cooper, the dog you've been talking about?"

Jane smiled. The dog plastered himself against her leg, and she reached down to pet the top of his head. "Yep. Mike ran into a problem with his landlady, and he couldn't keep him. So I offered to have him at Tides."

"Awesome. How do you like having a dog?"

"It's just temporary, but it is kind of nice having him around."

Maxi looked at the dog wistfully, but a pet wasn't in the cards for her right now. Her future suddenly felt uncertain. But this meeting was about Jane, not her. "So, tell me about this wedding. It's so exciting."

Jane took a deep breath. "I don't know if *exciting* is the word. *Terrifying* might be more like it. Someone emailed from that ad I took out in *Coastal Living*. Their wedding venue was canceled at the last minute, so they wanted to see if we were available. But the thing is the wedding is in less than five weeks."

"Five weeks? Can you pull a wedding together in that time?"

Jane shrugged. "I have no idea, but I'm going to try. They wanted a proposal and pictures of how it would be set up. I was hoping you could help me dress the place up a bit like it might be for a wedding."

Maxi surveyed the area, looking at the porch, the beach, the gardens. Her artistic eye immediately homed in on some things to highlight. "I think you can take an angle of the garden to show the new plants. Maybe use that bench and put some decorative pillows on it." Maxi turned to look at the porch. "And we can set up some tables on the porch here and put up those sheers and add some pillows." She turned again to face the ocean, framing a little picture in her hands with her thumb and forefinger. "And then take a picture of where you would set up the arbor. It's too bad we don't have that now."

"Maybe I can get Sally and Shane to work on that first. Andie is working on the garden. I could have her concentrate on one area so it will look nice for the picture."

"That sounds like a good plan. I can get some pillows, and we can have Sally tack up one sheer curtain, just so we can get it in the corner of one of the pictures.

Jane hugged her. "Thanks so much. I don't know what I would do without you and Claire."

"Same." At least Maxi could count on her friends. Even if things went wrong with James, she knew she'd have their support. She put her hand in her pocket, and her fingertips brushed the sharp edge of the business card she'd found in James's suit. It was Sandee Harris's card, and it had a phone number written in pen. Her business number was printed on the card, so Maxi assumed that must be a personal number. Why would James need that?

"Hey, remember when you asked if James and I were buying a cottage? Was that because you saw James with Sandee?"

Jane looked uneasy, her gaze drifting out to the ocean. "Well, I thought I did, but it was from far away. I was walking the beach and only saw them for a second. I think it was just someone who looked like James. Why do you ask?"

Images of James and Sandee and some illicit tryst in one of the cottages bubbled up. Maxi bent to pet Cooper so Jane couldn't see her face. "Oh, no reason, I was just curious."

She didn't want to voice her concerns, even to her

best friend. It was a big accusation to call someone a cheater, and she really had no proof other than the business card. If she was going to accuse James of cheating, she owed it to him to discuss it with him first.

A movement over at the garden caught her eye, and she turned to see Andie straightening up from the flower bed. She wiped her brow, smudging dirt on her face as she turned in their direction and waved.

Jane waved her over. "Perfect timing. Now we can ask her to concentrate on one area of the garden for the pictures."

Andie tugged off the hot, sweaty gardening gloves as she made her way toward Jane. She had to admit gardening was cathartic. It was satisfying to see the area come back to life with the colorful impatiens and lush, green hostas that she'd been planting.

"It's hot out here." Andie swiped at the sweat on her brow.

"The garden is looking great." Jane's kind words warmed her heart. "Maxi and I were just talking about taking pictures for the wedding client, and we were hoping you could concentrate on the area near the bench first."

"Wedding client?" Andie looked from Jane to Maxi. Had Jane gotten a bite on her ad?

"I didn't tell you?" Jane said. "Sorry, I just found out this morning. Someone emailed about having a wedding here. And they want pictures."

"That's great!" Andie was genuinely glad but a little worried about the amount of work. "It's a bit different from what we are used to, though."

"It is, but it will be good for Tides," Jane said. "It's just a small wedding, so I think we can pull it off."

"It will bring in good money. What can I do to help?" A look of surprise crossed Jane's face at Andie's offer. She supposed she couldn't blame her. Andie had never offered to get involved in the family business before, as she never stayed long enough. But for some reason, Andie felt this time was different. It wasn't just that Doug had apparently forgotten about her—it was something more. Her mother's words about the city not giving her what she really needed ran through her head.

"Thanks, I think the gardening will be a big help. I can handle everything else."

Andie nodded, a little disappointed that Jane hadn't called upon her for more, but why would she? She had Maxi and Claire, who were here to help all the time, and if the past was any indication, she probably thought that Andie was just passing through.

The French doors opened, and Chandler Vanbeck came out onto the porch. He stretched, inhaling deeply. "The sea air. Always so refreshing."

Maxi looked at him curiously, and Andie introduced them. As Maxi leaned forward to shake hands, the tote bag slipped off her arm and fell onto the deck, spilling its contents. Pencils rolled, sketchbooks flopped open, erasers bounced. Chandler bent down to help her pick them up. He hesitated when he saw one of her sketches. It was just a pencil sketch of a seagull, and Andie was no art expert, but even she could see that the details were exquisite, the shading so precise you almost expected the bird to fly off the page.

"This is wonderful." Chandler looked up at Maxi. "Are you the artist?"

"It's just a little sketch. It's nothing." Maxi snatched it from him and stuffed it in her bag, clearly embarrassed by the attention.

"Don't sell yourself short. You have talent." Chandler turned to Andie. "I was sorry to hear about the Richhaven job."

Andie frowned. "What about it?"

"You didn't hear? It came through, and Elise was named as the lead appraiser. She called me this morning to see if I could come out and appraise some of the artwork."

Andie felt as if she'd been punched in the gut. Elise had gotten the Richhaven job? That couldn't be possible. Doug had never even called her.

Chandler must've seen her look of disbelief because he continued, "I thought for sure you'd get it because you have so much more experience, but I guess I just assumed you're needed here and couldn't accept the job."

Jane and Maxi were looking at her. Could everyone sense how hurt she was?

"Right. It's more important for me to be here. My mom needs me right now." Andie started backing away. She had to get out of there before the tears that were threatening came. "Speaking of which, I better get going on the garden so you can get your pictures." She turned and hurried down the path to the garden.

In a daze, she sat on the stone bench and pulled out her phone. Maybe Doug had tried to message her about it. She'd been having so much fun focusing on the garden that she'd actually forgotten about him. She hadn't checked her messages in a while. But there was no message. No email. No text. No phone call. Doug had given the job to Elise without even consulting her.

Had they forgotten all about her at Christie's in the few days that she'd been out here? Maybe she should get back there right away to secure her job and make sure she didn't lose out on anything else. She could finish the section of the garden near the bench quickly, and Jane had made it perfectly clear that she didn't need any help here at Tides.

She scrolled to the airline site and started looking for flights.

ane spent the next few hours rearranging tables; tacking up soft, flowing, sheer drapes; and strategically placing pillows Maxi had picked up from the fabric store. Maxi instructed, and Jane took the pictures.

Shane and Sally were just starting on the arbor and dance floor, so she couldn't take pictures of those for a few days, but Jane wanted to get back to the client right away. She could send more pictures later.

By the time she was done, it was almost time for Mike to come and pick up Cooper. She took the laptop to the kitchen to organize the pictures and call the lobster-bake company and tent-rental place for quotes so that she could send that along with the pictures to the client.

She had to take all the expenses into consideration, but how much should she tack on for using Tides as the venue? Ten percent? Twenty? She had no idea what was reasonable but knew that wedding venues charged a high fee. Unfortunately, she didn't have a lot of time for research. She wanted the client to know that she was going to answer promptly and also really wanted to get that deposit in so that she could use it to pay the food-service people, who probably would not deliver food this week if she didn't pay.

She did her best and sent the email off with her fingers crossed. Part of her was terrified they would say yes, but the other part was getting a little excited about the wedding. It was all overshadowed by worry for her sister and Maxi.

Jane had no idea what the Richhaven job was but could guess it was something important. Andie had acted like the news that someone else had secured it was nothing, but Jane could tell her sister was pretty shaken about it. She'd wanted to go to the garden and see if she needed to talk about it, but she wasn't sure what to say or even if her efforts would be welcome. It wasn't like they'd had any heart-to-hearts in the last twenty years.

Jane had been surprised by Andie's offer to help with the wedding. She hadn't known what to say. Was

Andie planning on staying longer? She did seem serious about the garden, but Jane still wasn't sure whether she wanted to open her heart to letting her sister in only to be abandoned again.

And Maxi... why had she asked about seeing James with Sandee? Jane tried to remember exactly what she'd seen at the cottage that morning. She'd really only seen a glimpse and couldn't be absolutely certain that it had been James. The last thing she wanted was to jump to conclusions and cause a problem between James and Maxi.

Woof!

Cooper rushed to the back door, signaling Mike's arrival.

"Hey, boy, are you ready to go for a ride?" Mike asked.

Cooper spun in circles.

Jane laughed. "I guess you said the magic word."

"He does love rides." Mike clicked the leash to Cooper's collar, but instead of heading right to the door, he lingered at the end of the table.

"Have a good visit with your grandfather. Andie is there visiting my mom, so you might run into her," Jane said.

"I will." Mike still lingered, then at Jane's questioning look said, "I was thinking when we get back,

179

maybe you and I could take Cooper for a walk on the beach together. Since he's been staying at Tides, I haven't had much of a chance to walk him, and I noticed that you like to walk on the beach, too, so…"

Jane had been so busy with the wedding she'd forgotten that a big dog like Cooper needed exercise. Just another thing to learn about having a dog. "That sounds like a good idea. I should be done with my work by then."

Cooper wagged his tail faster, glancing between Mike and Jane as if he knew what they were talking about.

"Should I message you when I leave Tall Pines?" Mike pulled out his phone, and Jane realized they didn't even have each other's numbers.

"Right. Good idea." They exchanged contact info. It made Jane feel as if their relationship was taking a turn. Now Mike wasn't just some guy she ran into on the beach and hired to make her website. He was becoming a friend.

"Okay, it's a plan, then." Mike's eyes met hers, and Jane felt a little flutter in her stomach. As he left, Jane wondered if the walk was about more than just getting exercise for Cooper. Had Mike just asked her on some sort of date?

Shane and Sally had been working outside for hours, trying to finish the arbor and dance floor so Jane could take pictures. Jane decided to take them some lemonade and check on their progress.

Sally gulped down half the glass. "Thanks. It's hot out here."

Shane was a little more polite with his. He took a few sips and gestured to the work. "What do you think?"

Jane wasn't sure what she thought. All she saw were a few boards and part of a trellis. "I guess it's good progress."

"Yeah, the dance floor will go here." Sally picked up a stick and drew two very long lines in the sand. "Is that big enough?"

Jane nodded.

"And the arbor will be at the edge of the garden so that you can train the rosebushes to grow up it." Shane turned toward the ocean.

"And then when the bride and groom stand under it, they'll be facing the ocean, and the guests could be seated in folding chairs in the garden." Sally chugged the rest of her lemonade and then burped.

"Sounds wonderful," Jane said.

Sally smiled proudly. "Thanks. And then we can..." Sally paused midsentence, her gaze drifting past Jane's shoulder. She pulled a face. "Ugh."

Jane turned to see Sandee Harris stomping up the beach toward them.

"What's going on up here?" Sandee demanded.

"We're building a dance floor and an arbor for the new wedding venue," Sally said.

Sandee raised a perfectly plucked brow. "Wedding? You're having weddings here? You have to have permits for that, you know."

"I know." With all the excitement, Jane had forgotten about permits, but she wasn't about to tell Sandee that. She made a mental note to check into permits.

"And if you're doing anything on the beach, you need a special variance," Sandee said.

Jane crossed her arms over her chest. "That won't be a problem."

"How many guests?" Sandee asked.

"Small weddings, around fifty."

Sandee assessed the inn with narrowed eyes. "How many bathrooms do you have in there?"

"Each room has its own bathroom. My grandparents had it renovated that way for guest convenience decades ago."

Sandee clicked her tongue on the roof of her mouth and looked at Jane as if she'd just said something very stupid. "Not the *guest* rooms, the public space. If you're going to have weddings with fifty people, you'll need three bathrooms in the public areas of the venue."

Was that true? Jane jerked her gaze toward the house. "We only have one…"

"Well, that's going to be a problem." Sandee's voice held an air of superiority that grated on Jane. "And you won't be able to add more until the town meeting the middle of next month."

Jane's hopes plummeted. The wedding was before that.

"I suppose you could always bring in porta potties." Sandee wrinkled her nose, indicating her opinion of porta potties. "Well, good luck." She flounced off back toward the ocean, leaving them all staring after her.

Sally made a face at Sandee. "Don't listen to her. She's a killjoy."

But Jane was already starting to panic. She couldn't use porta potties—the client had specifically stated she didn't want that. Jane could've kicked herself. Why hadn't she thought about the bathroom situation?

The inn had ten rooms. If ten couples stayed here, that would be almost half the guests that would have their own private bathrooms. Would that waive the three-bathroom rule if several of them had their own? Would ten couples from the wedding even stay at the inn?

"Look, I wouldn't put much stock in what Sandee says," Shane said soothingly. "But even so, maybe you should go down to the town offices tomorrow and find out what the real story is."

Jane's phone pinged, and she pulled it out to see a text from her bank. "The wedding client made a deposit. I guess we're having a wedding."

"Holy smokes." Sally picked up her hammer and nails and headed toward the arbor. "We better get cracking. We only have a few weeks to get this place in shape."

Only a few weeks to line up caterers, tents, tables, flowers, and lord knew what else. Jane rushed back to her computer and got to work, assuring herself that the toilet situation was only a minor worry. Sandee probably just made all that up because she was mad that Jane didn't list Tides with her. At least now that she had some money, she could pay the food service. Of course, she'd need some to use for a deposit for the caterer and tent rental, but hopefully there would be some left she could funnel toward other bills. And if some of those wedding guests booked rooms, she'd get a small deposit and know that more was coming.

She was more than ready to take a break when Mike showed up with Cooper. As they set off down the beach, Jane was surprised to discover how much she'd been looking forward to their walk. She was really starting to get attached to Cooper, and Mike was good company.

They walked at a slow pace, and the conversation with simple and easy, like old friends'. *Just* friends, of course. Jane was sure that's all Mike was interested in. She actually felt embarrassed that the thought that he might have been asking her on a date had even crossed her mind. What was she thinking? She was old enough to be his... older sister. And that's probably exactly how he thought of her.

She glanced over at him as they walked. Sure, he was attractive, and she liked that he was tall—not many men were taller than her—but Mike didn't live here. He would be going back to Seattle, probably sooner rather than later. Jane had had enough of people that she cared about leaving her. She didn't want to get attached to someone else who would only be around for a short while. But being just *friends* while he was here couldn't be a bad thing, and besides, it was better for Cooper to have Mike around.

Mike watched Cooper bound after the piece of drift-wood he'd just tossed. The sea air was invigorating, the sun warm on his back, the water cold on his feet, and the company enchanting.

He and Jane walked along the edge of the surf, letting the water rush over their feet and up to their ankles. A shell caught his eye, and he bent to pick it up. It was a somewhat unusual shell—a squat brown-and-white spiral with a wide opening.

"Look at this. A basket whelk." He held the shell out in his palm.

"You know what that is?" Jane seemed surprised. "Most people just call that a snail shell."

"I've been interested in shells since I was a kid. I even found a fully intact purple dog whelk once when I was visiting Gramps years ago."

Jane glanced out into the ocean. "There used to be a lot more shells when we were kids. I used to comb the beach religiously for them every day. I got pretty good at identifying them."

"Me too," Mike said. "It's kind of sad that there's not as many shells anymore. Where do you think they've all gone? And the sea glass too. There used to be tons of it in all different colors."

"I remember." Jane bent and picked something out of the surf. She held it out in the palm of her hand. It was a smooth, round shell in a bland beige, just shy of being luminescent. "What's this one?"

Mike took it from her and turned it over in his hand. There were several types of shells that were similar in shape and size and color, but Mike knew the subtle differences. "That's easy—this is a Northern moon snail."

Jane laughed. "I guess I can't trip you up."

"Nope." Mike handed the shell back to her, noticing how her nose crinkled and her blue eyes lit up when she laughed. She seemed less stressed than usual. Maybe it was being out at the beach, but he liked to think it had something to do with him. Probably more to do with Cooper, though.

As they sauntered along the edge of the beach, he resisted the urge to grab her hand. He wasn't sure if that would be welcome. He thought it might be, but he didn't want to do anything to ruin their blossoming friendship.

Cooper ran up and dropped a stick at their feet then proceeded to shake his wet coat, spraying drops of salt-water everywhere.

"Look out!" Jane and Mike both held up their hands, and Mike stepped in front of her to try to shield her from the onslaught.

It didn't work, and they were both covered with

droplets. Jane didn't get mad, like some other girls he knew. She didn't whine about her hair or makeup being ruined. She simply laughed and rubbed Cooper's neck.

"You know, Cooper has a way of making one forget about their troubles. He lives in the moment and always has fun," Jane said.

"That's not a bad way to be," Mike said. "So, what's going on with the wedding at Tides?"

"Didn't I tell you? They sent in their deposit."

"That's great!" Mike glanced at Jane, but instead of looking happy about the wedding, she looked tense. "You don't seem very happy about that."

Jane sighed. "The truth is I'm a little worried about it. I've never taken on anything this big, and there may be a snag with permits."

"What kind of snag?"

Jane waved her hand dismissively. "Something about the bathrooms, but the person who mentioned that isn't exactly reliable. I'll know more when I talk to the people at the town hall. It's probably nothing."

"I'm sure that whatever it is, you can handle it."

Jane smiled and glanced at him. "I appreciate your confidence in me, but you don't know me that well. I like to stay in my comfort zone, so this is all scary territory for me."

"I know enough to know that you're confident and

capable. You're going to do fine. And besides, sometimes it's good to get out of your comfort zone, don't you think?"

Jane hesitated for a minute, as if thinking it over. "I don't know. Maybe you're right."

Mike decided to steer the conversation toward something that would give Jane a positive outlook on the wedding. "I'm going to have your website finished tonight."

"Already? That's great! I don't feel like I paid you enough for that, though," Jane said.

"You might want to wait until you see it before you say that. I'll come over for breakfast tomorrow and walk you through it. You might decide it's not worth a few breakfasts."

Jane laughed. "I doubt that."

"Besides, you're keeping Cooper, and that's worth a lot. You know what it would cost to put him in the kennel?"

Jane glanced at Cooper. "Having him around is my pleasure. But you can still come for breakfast every day for as long as you're in Lobster Bay. I owe you at least that much."

Mike glanced over and tried to read her face, but she was looking away from him toward the ocean. Did she really want him to come for payment, or did she like his company? "Home-cooked breakfasts are always welcome, but you don't need to do that. Are you sure?"

"Yes, of course. We have plenty of food."

"Okay, then I guess I won't look a gift horse in the mouth."

Jane smiled and tossed a piece of driftwood for Cooper. "Cooper will be very happy about that."

CHAPTER 20

The next day, Jane helped Brenda with breakfast. Even though they only had two guests and Mike to feed—and Brenda could surely manage that on her own—Jane sometimes liked to help, as the familiar task of cooking breakfast helped her think.

"We might have a full inn again with this wedding. I'm going to need a lot of eggs and bacon." Jane took care not to splatter her hand as she flipped over the pieces of bacon that sizzled in her grandmother's cast-iron pan. "I've booked the Lobster Bay Clambake Company for the wedding, so we don't have to worry about cooking food for that." Good thing, too, as the kitchen was much too small to provide the types of meals that a wedding would require. If they were going to do weddings, they would all have to be catered.

Brenda soaked a thick piece of bread in the egg mixture she'd just mixed. "I might come up with some different dishes for breakfast. Maybe something fancier."

Jane glanced at Brenda. New dishes? Tides had served the same things for breakfast for as long as she could remember. Then again, maybe fancier dishes would bring in more people. She thought back to Mike's comment about getting out of her comfort zone. That applied to the small things as well. "Like what?"

"I don't know. Eggs Benedict, quiche, breakfast sandwiches."

"That does sound good. Maybe I should do some research and see what other inns offer."

Brenda sliced off a chunk of butter and put it in another cast-iron frying pan, watching it melt. "Andie has already been down to eat. I told her to wait for a hot breakfast, but she grabbed a muffin and took it back to her room."

Jane frowned. "Really? Was she not feeling well?"

Brenda picked up the egg-soaked bread with tongs and laid it in the puddle of butter. "She didn't say much. Seemed a little down in the dumps."

It was probably that job she'd lost. Maybe Jane should've gone to her and said something to make her feel better. But now Jane had to wonder... if Andie's job wasn't so good back in New York City, would staying in Lobster Bay appeal to her?

Andie had offered to help with the inn, but were those just hollow words? Jane battled the urge to ask her sister to stay. What if Andie said no? Jane wasn't quite ready to open herself up to disappointment. Still, maybe she should run up there and see if Andie was okay. But Mike would be here any minute to show her the website. Maybe after that she could talk to Andie.

Jane's thoughts were interrupted by a knock on the kitchen door. Outside stood a man in a suit holding a clipboard.

She went to the door and stood on the threshold. "Can I help you?"

The man stuck out his hand. "Hi, I'm Bob Grover from the Lobster Bay town offices. No one was in the lobby, so I figured I'd find you out back in the kitchen anyway."

Jane's stomach tightened even as she smiled at him and motioned for him to come into the kitchen. "What can I do for you?"

"I heard you're planning a wedding here, and I've

come to check your facilities and make sure you have the appropriate permits."

"Where did you hear that?"

"I got a note on my desk." Bob smiled. "It might seem a little informal, but that's the way things happen here in Lobster Bay. Is this a bad time?"

Jane doubted someone randomly found out about the wedding and put a note on Bob's desk. No one knew about it except her friends, Andie, Mike, Shane, and Sally. None of them would go to the town hall. Jane knew exactly where the information had come from. Sandee Harris. It was no coincidence she had been blathering on about permits just yesterday. But why would Sandee try to ruin things for Jane? Was she purposely trying to make it so that Tides would fail so she could scoop it up at a cheap price?

"Not at all. What do you need to see?"

Jane walked Bob through the inn, showing him the main gathering area, the porch, and where everything would be set up outside.

"So, you won't be cooking for the guests in the kitchen here, then?" Bob asked.

"No. We're not set up for that. It's going to be a catered lobster bake."

"And the only structures are the portable dance floor and arbor?"

"Yep."

Bob jotted something on his clipboard. "Okay, then. Looks like you don't need a building permit, and since you're not using the kitchen, there's nothing to inspect there." Bob pressed his lips together. "I'm not sure why this landed on my desk. I think you just need a variance for the clambake and gathering on the beach, but that's no problem. You can see Mary down at the town offices and get one today."

Jane had an idea why it had landed on his desk. Sandee was trying to make trouble. But that had backfired, as Bob had given the inn his blessing, and it wouldn't be any problem to get the variance.

"Great. Thanks for coming." Jane started walking toward the driveway, but Bob paused and turned. "How many guests did you say this wedding was going to have?"

Jane's hopes sank. "About forty to fifty."

Bob turned toward the inn. "And how many public bathrooms do you have in there?"

"Well, there are ten bathrooms, but those are with the rooms. The common area has one because every room has its own private bathroom."

Bob rifled through a battered codebook. "That doesn't matter. Even if the rooms are booked. Page fifty-six, section seventy-three, subsection A of the beach-gathering code says you have to have one toilet for every thirty guests at a gathering." He looked up from the book, apologetic. "So that means you're going to need another toilet. Of course, you can get Clean Day to bring some porta potties."

Shoot! Porta potties wouldn't do. "Maybe I could add a real bathroom…" She glanced around over at the inn. Where could she carve out some space for another bathroom? Off the living room? Maybe close off part of the porch? "How long would it take to add a bathroom?"

Bob shook his head. "I don't think you can add one. That takes a special meeting with the town sewer-and-water committee. Because the property is on the beach, there are special considerations, and they don't meet until next month. No exceptions there. Sorry, but you're only allowed as many bathrooms as the house originally had or were added before 1953."

Jane wanted to cry. She'd been getting her hopes up, thinking this wedding could solve all her financial problems, but now it looked like she might have to refund the deposit money that she'd already spent.

"I'm very sorry," Bob said.

"It's not your fault." Jane walked him up to the driveway, her hopes sinking even further. As if sensing her mood, Cooper pressed himself against her for comfort.

"Morning!" Jane turned to see Mike coming up the beach toward them. Cooper ran to him and did his tail-wagging routine.

Mike petted the dog, then his eyes filled with concern as he looked at Jane. "What's wrong?"

She told him about Bob's visit and the distressing news about the bathrooms.

He put his hand on her arm. It was warm and comforting. "That can't be right. There's got to be something you can do."

Jane sighed. "I don't know. It seemed pretty cut-and-dried. He made it pretty clear that the committee doesn't meet until next month, and the wedding is supposed to be in almost four weeks. Even if the meeting is the week before, it's not enough time. I can't keep the client hanging on, as they'd need to find another venue as soon as possible. It's almost impossible to get something last minute."

Mike pressed his lips together. "Let's not give up. There's got be a way. We just need time to think about it."

"Maybe." Mike's words gave Jane a little encouragement. Maybe he was right and there was a way to work this out.

But what was this "we" stuff? He didn't need to make this his problem. Determined to think positive, she brightened. "Either way, I'm going to need a website, so let's go inside and see what this thing looks like."

CHAPTER 21

*A*ndie's grip tightened on the phone as she listened to Susie fill her in on everything that had been happening at work.

"And Elise has been spending a lot of time in Doug's office," Susie whispered into the phone after verifying that Elise had gotten the lead-appraiser position on the Richhaven job.

Andie used to spend a lot of time in Doug's office, too, but surprisingly the fact that she'd been cast aside for Elise didn't bother her at all. Her feelings for Doug had evaporated with his shoddy treatment. "Is there anything else going on? Any rumors of new jobs coming in?"

"Nope. Dull as a doornail here… whoops, I gotta go. Marcy is looking for me."

They hung up, and Andie glanced at the airline app on her phone, where she'd made a reservation for a flight for the next day.

It was time she headed back to New York City. If she didn't do anything to protect her job, she might end up as the low person on the totem pole. But unlike her previous visits to Lobster Bay, this time she was in no rush to get back. Maybe after all these years, the excitement of antiques appraisal had worn off. If she hadn't made that exciting find yet, what were the odds it would come along now? It wasn't like her career had been unsatisfying. There had been plenty of exciting small finds over the years.

Outside her window, the sunlight sparkled on the tops of the waves. Her visit to Lobster Bay had been a great change of pace from the city. It was slower here, less hectic. There were no interoffice politics, no married bosses. If only there was more to do in this town—something she could sink her teeth into. Something that gave her a purpose.

She'd enjoyed working in the garden more than she'd thought possible. Speaking of which, she didn't want to leave it half finished. She'd have to get a move on if she wanted to complete the garden and visit her mother at Tall Pines before her flight tomorrow.

Standing, she stretched and made her way downstairs, creeping down the stairs slowly and peeking over the railing to make sure she didn't run into Shane Flannery. One good thing about leaving tomorrow was that it would ensure that she wouldn't have to see him again.

Jane was in the living room, staring at the wall of paintings that Chandler Vanbeck had said were so valuable. "Hey, sis, I…"

Jane turned, and Andie could sense that something was wrong. "Is something the matter?"

Jane shrugged. "I think we might have to sell one of these paintings after all. If you'll agree."

Andie's eyes flicked to the painting, a seascape with turbulent waves crashing on jagged rocks.

"What? Why?" She had a sinking feeling that the finances were a lot worse than her sister had let on. She'd felt something was off all along and should've insisted that Jane give her specifics, but she'd felt like it was none of her business. Jane had been taking care of this all along, and Andie was ashamed that she'd never once offered to help or asked how things were going. Who was she to butt in now?

Jane sighed. "I'm afraid the wedding might not happen. We have to put in a new bathroom to accommodate all the guests."

"Oh. Well, that seems problematic, but why do we

need to sell a painting because the wedding is off? Are finances that bad?"

Jane looked as if she might cry, and Andie resisted the urge to hug her, not sure if the gesture would be welcome.

"I'm sorry. I guess I should've fessed up sooner. I just didn't want you to think that I'd ruined the family business, but the truth is finances are not okay. This wedding was going to bail us out," Jane said.

"Ruin the family business? I never would've thought that." Andie felt like a selfish jerk. How could things have gotten so messed up between them that Jane felt like Andie would blame her for ruining the business instead of knowing she would jump in to help her?

Plagued with guilt over leaving everything on Jane's shoulders, Andie was moved to solve the problem. "Okay, so the client doesn't want porta potties. Who could blame them? But could we add another bathroom?" Andie mentally added up the money in her 401(k). She could take some out—the heck with the penalty. Her sister needed her help, and that was more important.

"Where would we put it? The space is tight down here. Even if we could add another one, would we get it done in time for the wedding? And how would we pay for it? Not to mention that we need to wait for some special approval that we can only get during a meeting that doesn't happen until next month." Jane flapped her arms. "It's hopeless."

"Can you request an emergency meeting? What about the upstairs bathrooms? We have plenty of those." Andie couldn't believe how backward things were in these small towns.

"Those bathrooms go with the guest rooms, so they don't count. According to the man from the town hall, if we put in more bathrooms than the house originally had or were added when plumbing came along, then we need some special variance."

Standing there with her sister, surrounded by their family belongings and the ocean in the background, she could feel the memories bubbling up. How many times had she stood here with her sister? Her mother? Her grandmother?

This house was full of those memories. She should have read between the lines and realized things were this bad, but she had been too involved in her own problems. Suddenly, Andie realized that more than anything, she wanted Tides to prosper. More than her job back at Christie's, more than being part of a significant antiques find. She felt a sudden closeness with Jane that she hadn't felt since they were kids. Jane needed her. And not only that, but something about what Jane had just said sparked an idea in her brain.

"Wait a minute! Did you say something about the original bathrooms?" Andie asked.

"Yeah, I guess there's something grandfathered in. But this place didn't have bathrooms originally, remember? Gramps added them with his father when indoor plumbing took off."

"I remember. They had to reconfigure some bedrooms to turn it into an inn with private baths for every room," Andie said. "I'm not sure, though. All might not be lost yet."

"I doubt that. The guy was pretty sure that we couldn't get a special meeting." Jane cocked her head and squinted at Andie. "Was there something you wanted to talk to me about?"

"It was nothing." Andie spun on her heel and started walking away. "Don't cancel the wedding or do anything drastic until you talk to me."

"Why? What are you going to do?"

"I'll tell you later tonight! Until then, keep the faith."

As Andie hurried out to her car, she opened the air-travel app on her phone and canceled the plane ticket. She didn't want to say anything to Jane because she didn't want to get her hopes up, but if Andie's plan worked, Jane was going to need her help for this wedding—and maybe even beyond.

The drama with the bathrooms had made Jane and Cooper late for the weekly meeting with Maxi and Claire at Sandcastles. She'd walked from Tides because she needed the time to think, not only about the bathroom situation but also about Andie's parting words. What in the world was she up to?

Maxi and Claire were already seated at a table on the sidewalk with a tray of pastries and mugs of coffee in front of them when she got there. They were midconversation, talking animatedly and gesturing. Jane slipped into a chair, and Cooper flopped down at her feet.

"And we can make the sandcastle cake with the colored frosting to match the wedding colors." Claire slid the tray of pastries over toward Jane. "Don't you think that would be great, Jane? Add a personal touch?"

"And I was thinking I could make a few special pillows to match the wedding party. It would bring all the decor together and make the weddings at Tides really special," Maxi added. "We could place them on the rockers on the back porch."

Her friends were so excited about the wedding that Jane almost didn't have the heart tell them about the bathroom problem. "Those sound like great ideas, but I'm afraid there might not be a wedding. At least not this summer."

Their faces fell. "What? Why?"

Jane told them about her visit with Bob and the issue with the bathrooms. "The client specified no porta potties, so I'm not sure what to do. I can email them and see if they'll make an exception given the tight schedule, but she seemed pretty adamant."

"There must be something we can do," Claire said.

Jane picked a pistachio muffin off the tray and broke it in half. "Andie said she had some kind of idea, but she wouldn't say what it was, so I don't know if it's anything good."

Claire pursed her lips. "Well, at least she's trying to help now."

Maxi patted Jane's hand. "Don't give up. Something else will come along."

Jane sighed. "I know. It's just disappointing." She bit into the muffin and chewed for a few seconds. "At least I have a good website now."

"Oh? So Mike made the website? I'll have to check that out. He did a good job?"

"Yep. He put in everything I wanted and did it

really quick too." Jane bent down and patted Cooper's head. "Thing is, he won't take any payment. Just breakfast every morning at the inn."

Claire and Maxi exchanged a look.

"He's been coming over every morning?" Maxi leaned forward. "Tell us more."

"There's nothing really to tell." Clearly Maxi thought there was more going on between her and Mike, and Jane wasn't sure how to address that. Jane suddenly felt flustered, tongue-tied.

Luckily, Hailey saved Jane from having to answer more questions. As she carefully stepped over Cooper to top off their coffees, Maxi's attention switched to the young single mother.

"Hailey, I was cleaning out some of the closets at home, and I found these old toys from when my daughters were kids." Maxi rummaged in her giant tote bag, pulling out pencils, sketches, notebooks, erasers. Finally, she pulled out a little pink gift bag and presented it to Hailey. "Do you think Jennifer would like them?"

Hailey peered into the bag. "Yes, she loves dolls. That's so nice of you to think of her."

Maxi shrugged. "Well, it's not like my girls are going to use them, and I hate to see them go to waste."

Maxi's expression was somber. Why was she

cleaning out her house? Jane knew that her friend cherished the childhood memories of her kids and was surprised to see her giving things away. Though she supposed one couldn't hold on to that stuff forever, and it wasn't unusual for her to bring gifts for Jennifer. Maybe it helped Maxi not feel so much like her nest was empty to know that the dolls went to good use.

Maxi started putting things back in her bag, and Jane saw that as the perfect opportunity to take the focus off herself. She turned to Claire. "Did Maxi tell you what my new guest, Chandler Vanbeck, said about her sketches?"

Claire looked at Maxi. "No? Who is Chandler Vanbeck, and when did he see your sketches?"

Maxi waved her hand dismissively. "It's nothing. They fell out of my bag when I was at Tides trying to come up with ideas for the wedding."

"It's not nothing," Jane said. "Andie said that Chandler is a renowned art critic. He saw Maxi's sketch and said it was quite good."

Claire sipped her coffee. "Well, that's no surprise. We all know Maxi is a fantastic artist."

"Oh, come on! It was just a rough sketch. He was probably just trying to be nice." Maxi tried to brush it off as if it was nothing, but Jane got this feeling that she was actually pleased and proud.

"I think you should do something with your artwork. Maybe have an art show or something. Don't you think, Claire?" Jane turned to look at Claire, but her friend's attention was riveted on something behind Jane. Jane turned to see Rob Bradford coming over from his bread store across the street.

"Hi, ladies," Rob said, his kind smile lighting his face. He nodded to Jane and Maxi, and then his eyes locked on Claire as if she were the Hope Diamond. He skirted around the plants, came over to the table, and kissed her on the cheek, causing her face to turn scarlet.

"Hi, Rob. How's the bread business?" Maxi asked.

"Pretty good. I was just going out to run some errands. Do you need anything, Claire?"

"No, thanks."

Rob raised his brows at Jane and Maxi. "Anyone else?"

"Nope, I'm good," Maxi said.

"Me too," Jane added.

"Okay, I'll leave you ladies to your coffee." Rob walked off, hands in his pockets, whistling.

"He comes over and asks if you need errands run?" Maxi said. "Looks like things are really cooking up with him."

Claire squirmed primly in her chair. "He was just being neighborly."

"Yeah, sure," Maxi said. "No matter how you slice it, I think there's some heat in the kitchen."

Jane sipped her coffee, enjoying Claire's discomfort. It was hilarious that she was pretending her relationship with Rob was no big deal but couldn't wipe the smile off her face. "I can't blame you, Claire. Rob's a nice guy, and the fact that he knows how to cook is just the icing on top."

"Okay, guys. Stop!" Claire waved her hands, and they all burst out laughing.

Jane's heart lifted. Her friends were happy and doing well. She'd been a bit worried about Maxi, but looking at her now, there was nothing to worry about. Surely that person she'd seen at the cottage with Sandee really hadn't been James. It was all just her imagination.

Everyone was doing good... except her. Jane's gaze dropped to her muffin, and she shoved another piece in her mouth, remembering how she'd used the deposit for the wedding to pay for the food delivery. If she canceled the wedding, she'd have to give the deposit back. Where would she get the money for that?

Hopefully, whatever Andie was up to would pan out. It was her only hope.

CHAPTER 22

The finances looked grim. Jane had tried jiggling this and moving that, but every way she looked at it, she came up short. The pinging of her phone with a text from Mike was a welcome distraction.

Can I pick up Cooper to visit Gramps?

Jane could use a break, so she messaged back suggesting she join them. She was due to visit her mother.

"Why don't you come in and meet Gramps real quick?" Mike asked as they walked into the foyer of Tall Pines.

"Okay. I guess it would be nice to know some of the other residents."

Mike led the way, and as they passed the locked

door that led to the dementia wing, his face softened. "I'm sorry that your mom is in the dementia section. That must be hard. At least Gramps is still fairly sharp. He forgets stuff every once in a while and has trouble with self-care, but I'm grateful he's not worse."

Jane's hand automatically felt for the comfort of Cooper's head. "Thanks. It's hard sometimes, but she can be lucid at times. I have to hang on to that. She seems to like it here, so that's a relief." Jane pushed away thoughts of how the money would run out in six months if she didn't find a way to get Tides profitable.

When they got closer to Gramps's room, Cooper sped up, running in ahead of them.

Mike and Jane got to the door in time to see his grandfather bent over, petting the dog, a look of pure joy on his face. Mike's grandfather was a thin man with a wrinkled, weathered face and a full head of silvery hair.

"Have you been a good boy?" Gramps asked, happily accepting Cooper's kisses. He glanced up at them. "Hi, Michael." His gaze drifted to Jane. "Who is this?"

Jane stepped in and held out her hand. "Jane Miller."

He put his hand in hers. It was worn and calloused but warm and friendly. "George Henderson." His eyes drifted to Mike. "I see you finally found yourself someone suitable."

"Oh no. We're not..." Jane looked from George to Mike, not knowing what to say.

"Cooper is staying with Jane. And Jane's mother is here in the dementia wing, so we decided to come together," Mike said.

"Oh, I see." George's eyes twinkled, and he winked at Mike, as if not quite believing his explanation. Then he cocked his head to the side and looked at Jane. "Did you say your last name was Miller? Are you from Lobster Bay?"

Jane had kept her maiden name even when she'd been married. Though Miller was a common name, her family was well-known in Lobster Bay, and she was proud of it.

"Yes. My family has owned Tides, the inn on the beach, for generations."

"Yes... yes. I knew your grandparents. Frank and Delta, right? Frank did me a big favor once. I'll never forget that," George said.

"That sounds like Gramps," Jane said proudly. Her grandparents and her parents were all about helping people when they could. "Well, I'll let you two visit." She turned to Mike. "Should I meet you in the lobby?"

"Yeah. How does an hour sound?" Mike asked.

"Sounds good." Jane took off back toward the dementia wing.

Mike was lucky his grandfather still had his memories, but she was lucky, too, because Addie still remembered *sometimes*. Jane had seen that some of the other patients here were much, much worse, and she decided to be grateful for what she had.

Her mother was in her room this time, asleep in the chair with a book in her hand. She looked peaceful, like a child without any worries. Perhaps that was what she was. Maybe being in the state that she was in and being well cared for wasn't so bad after all. The painting she'd seen Addie doing the other day was hanging on the wall, fresh laundry sat folded on top of the bureau, and the room was clean.

"You watch out for that one." A woman with a walker was approaching from the other end of the hall. "She's got sticky fingers."

"Sticky fingers?" Jane asked.

"Steals things." The woman stopped at the door. "In fact, I think she has my sweater."

The woman started into the room. Just then a nurse came along and grabbed her gently by the elbow. "Now, Sadie, come along. Didn't you want to go to the puzzle room?"

Sadie scowled at the nurse. "Puzzle room? Oh yeah.

I did. That's right. I'm working on that piece with the moose in it."

She let the nurse lead her away. As they were walking down the hall, Jane heard her ask, "Say, have you seen my sweater with the seashell buttons?"

Addie had been awakened by the noise, and she smiled at Jane benignly. Jane's stomach swooped. Addie didn't recognize her.

"Hello," Addie said in her polite tone reserved for strangers.

"Hi." Jane stepped over to the painting and pointed at it. "This is a lovely painting. Did you do it?"

Addie smiled proudly. "Yes. Do you see how I made the highlights and contrasted the colors?"

"I do." Jane noticed the lunch tray on her desk. "Did you have a good lunch? What was it today?"

Addie frowned, as if trying to remember, then she brightened. "Oh yes, it was very good. Hot dogs. I like mine a bit crispier, but what can you do? The service in this hotel isn't like the Park Plaza."

Jane sat on the end of the bed, and her mother put the book aside. "Now, was there something you wanted to talk to me about? You'll have to make it quick. We have a sing-along before supper, and I don't want to miss it."

CHAPTER 23

axi stared at the ocean beyond the wall of glass windows in her living room. It was suppertime, and the summer sun was low in the sky, bouncing off the waves and turning the sail on the boat in the distance bright white. What color blue would she use to capture that scene if she were painting. Cerulean? No, it was lighter. Maybe manganese with a touch of green.

She turned away from the window, her thoughts turning to her friend. Jane had talked a good talk at Sandcastles that morning, but Maxi could see she was worried about Tides. Jane needed the money from the wedding to keep Tides going. Jane wouldn't burden Maxi or Claire with her problems, but Maxi wished there was some way she could help. Maybe she could approach James about giving Jane a low-interest loan. *If James ever came home.* These days he hardly ever showed up for dinner.

As if trying to prove her a liar, the front door opened. He smiled when he saw her, just like old times. It was as if nothing was wrong, which made Maxi wonder if something actually was wrong or if it was all her imagination.

"Hey, honey." As he walked toward her, she was struck by how handsome he was. Over the last years, he'd gained a few wrinkles, a couple of extra pounds, and some gray hair, but he still made her heart beat faster, just like he had when they'd first met. He came over and kissed her cheek, the spicy smell of his aftershave bringing up all kinds of emotions. Funny, he wasn't acting like a man who was having an affair.

"Something smells great. What's for supper?"

"Pot roast." Maxi wasn't sure why she still cooked big meals. With the kids gone and James working late most nights, it was usually a waste. But old habits die hard. Or was she just desperate to have things return to the way they were before?

He looked pleased. "My favorite. Roasted potatoes too?"

Maxi nodded. "The way you like them."

"Can I help you with anything?" He took his jacket

off, folded it precisely, then laid it over the back of the sofa.

"I guess you could set the table." Maxi didn't bother setting the table anymore, since she never knew if he would be home.

She followed him to the kitchen and checked on the potatoes while he pulled out plates, silverware, and glassware.

"How was your day?" he asked as he meticulously placed the items on the modern granite table.

"Great. You?" *Did you inspect any beach cottages with Sandee Harris?*

James shrugged. "Boring. You want wine?"

"Sure."

They ate, settling into the familiar routine, just like thousands of meals they'd eaten before. It was as if nothing was wrong, and Maxi again wondered if she was just being overly sensitive. Emboldened by their closeness, or maybe by the wine, she asked, "I was wondering, were you at one of the beach cottages the other day?"

James glanced away, taking a sip of wine. "The cottages? No. Why would I be at a cottage?"

Maxi studied him for a second, her heart breaking. After thirty years, she knew all his tells. James was lying.

"Oh, no reason." She focused on her pot roast, trying to keep tears at bay as she moved the pieces from one side of the plate to the other. Her appetite was gone. An awkward silence fell.

Why hadn't she asked him point-blank about Sandee? What was wrong with her? Didn't she have the guts to confront him?

But she had no evidence. Even Jane was now saying that it wasn't James that she'd seen. And a business card was hardly proof of anything. What if she accused him and was wrong? Infidelity was a pretty serious accusation, and it would definitely put a wedge between them. No, she'd watch and wait until she could get solid evidence. Meanwhile, she'd use the time to get all her ducks in a row, make sure he didn't control the finances so he could cut her out.

Once she had evidence and things were set so that she'd come out of this with her fair share, she *would* confront him. She had no intention of turning into one of those wives who just ignored her husband's infidelities.

CHAPTER 24

"I'm almost done with these spindles on the main stairs. What do you think?" Sally stood back, admiring her handiwork.

Jane was impressed. The turnings in the spindles matched exactly. "Nice job."

"Shane helped."

"Seems like he's doing great work." Jane turned back to the paintings she'd been studying. They were similar to the ones in the living room and just as old. They did have a lot of them, and maybe if they had to sell just one, it wouldn't be so bad.

"Ah-yuh." Sally lingered instead of going back to work. "Those are nice paintings. Always liked those."

"Me too. Chandler Vanbeck said the ones in the living room are really valuable."

Sally scowled. "You're not thinking of selling them?"

"We might have to. Without another bathroom, the wedding will probably fall through, and we're running low on funds." Jane hated to admit it, but she supposed she was going to have to say it out loud at some point.

"Didn't Andie say she had a plan?" Sally asked.

Did Sally hear everything that went on around the inn?

"Yeah, but then she took off, and I haven't heard from her."

Sally started picking up her tools. "Have some faith. That girl will come around. You'll see."

Jane turned back to the painting. She wasn't so sure about that. If Andie followed her usual pattern, she was probably booking a flight back to New York right now.

The front door flew open, and Andie rushed in. "Big news! I've just been to the town hall. I talked to the building inspector, the town clerk, even the town attorney."

"And?" Jane asked. Andie's face was flushed with excitement, her body nervous with energy.

"It turns out that we can put two more bathrooms in, and we don't need a special variance." Andie fist-bumped Sally then turned to Jane, her fist out.

Jane was skeptical but bumped knuckles with her anyway. "We can? How did you wrangle that?"

"I didn't really have to wrangle anything. Something you said about the existing bathrooms triggered a thought in my mind. Remember the three-seater outhouse that we use for storage?"

"Yeah, I remember we used to play there as kids. Yuck. But it's all run-down and gross. It's worse than a porta potty. That will never fly with the wedding client."

"We're not going to use the outhouse. The town clerk said that you needed a special variance if you wanted to add more than the *existing* bathrooms. Well, come to find out those bathrooms in the outhouse count as existing."

"They do?" Jane was having a hard time believing it could be this easy. "But they're not hooked up to plumbing or anything."

"Doesn't matter. It's a loophole because the bathrooms existed originally with the house. I've run into similar things in my business. Not with bathrooms but with existing laws and things grandfathered in. That's what made me think of it." Andie pulled a piece of paper out of her bag. "I have the permit to renovate the outhouse with a functioning bathroom right here. No special variance necessary."

Jane's spirits lifted. On impulse, she hugged Andie. It was a little awkward and stiff, but it was a start. "That's great news. We can still have the wedding. Shoot! Except... how can we build an entire bathroom structure in four weeks?"

"I bet we could do it in two weeks with the right people," Sally piped up. "We built one for the Andersons in eight days."

Jane was still doubtful. "Seriously? Where would we find people to work on it on such short notice?"

Sally winked. "I know a lot of people in this town that don't want to see Tides go under. Your grandparents helped their grandparents, and they'll be happy to repay the favor. Lord knows what they would build here if you had to sell, and no one wants some new monstrosity coming in. With a little bit of persuasion and a few favors, people will be able to shuffle their schedules around."

Jane couldn't believe it. "Do you really think so?"

"Ah-yuh. And I know we can persuade Ralph Marchand to do the plumbing. Good thing Claire already greased the skids with him by plying him with all those free pastries when he was fixing the pipes at Sandcastles."

CHAPTER 25

*T*he next week flew by in a blur of permit getting, supply ordering, and contractor hiring. Before Jane knew it, the old outhouse building had been cleaned out and demolished. A backhoe had dug a hole for the foundation of the small bath building that would replace it, and concrete had been poured.

The design of the bath building was simple, but the white siding and nautical-blue trim would match with Tides. Things couldn't have worked out more perfectly because this separate bathroom would come in handy if Jane had events out in the garden. People wouldn't have to traipse back into the inn this way, and Andie had suggested adding a planting bench with a sink and a foot-wash station for people coming from the beach on one side.

Maxi and Andie had bonded over coming up with the design for the bathroom. Jane was happy to leave it to them. They'd taken several trips to the local home-fixer-upper store, picking out toilets and sinks and fixtures. Andie had even managed to get a coupon so everything could be bought at a discount.

Thankfully, a second wedding deposit came in, and wedding guests were booking rooms at the inn for the days surrounding the wedding.

The project was expensive, though, so Jane had taken out a small equity line of credit on Tides, thanks to Maxi and James, who had pushed it through quickly for her. The interest rate on a line of credit was much lower than a regular loan, and it was faster to get and better than charging things on credit cards.

Jane was heartened by the way people had juggled their schedules to accommodate her. Many of the local business owners had taken over the businesses from their parents, who had been friends of Jane's parents. And they all wanted to help their neighbor.

The permits had been sped through the system. Shane and Sally had worked double time on the bathroom, arbor, and dance floor. Jane suspected they weren't even charging her for some of their hours. Claire had made some extra pastries to bribe Ralph

Marchand to drop what he was doing and plumb the building as soon as they were ready.

Jane stood with her feet planted in the sand and Cooper at her side, watching workers nail down the roofing on the small building. She could hardly believe it was really happening.

Woof!

Cooper bounded off to meet Mike, who was walking up the beach toward Tides. He'd texted earlier to see if he could take Cooper to visit his grandfather at Tall Pines and had invited her to go with them, but she had so much to do here that she couldn't go.

"Things are really coming along. Looks like you'll be able to have the wedding after all." Mike was clearly happy for her, but Jane's excitement dimmed a little. There was still one fly in the ointment.

"Maybe. There is one problem. We still need to hook up to the sewer lines at the street, and for that we need the town sewer people to come out. We've almost got everything ready for them, but they have a full schedule, and it might take several weeks before they can fit us in. They said they'd call if there was a cancellation, but there's a chance we might not be able to get the bathroom up and running in time."

Mike frowned. "You've come this far. Something

like that can't stop you now. Are all the other plans moving forward?"

Jane nodded. "Wedding guests are already starting to book rooms for that weekend. Maxi is making special pillows. Claire is matching the cake to the bridesmaids' dresses. It would be a tragedy if I had to call it off now. I mean, not only will it be bad for Tides, but these poor people will never be able to book another venue in time." Jane sighed, feeling the weight of ruining someone's wedding on her shoulders. They had a few weeks before the wedding, but Jane would feel a lot better if the bathrooms were up and running now. What if something happened to delay the completion and she had to cancel at the last minute? That would surely result in some bad reviews.

Mike put a hand on her arm. "Don't worry. You still have a few weeks. And besides, I think I might be able to help."

"How?"

"Leave that to me."

As Jane watched him leave, she realized that Mike and Cooper might not be around much longer. She'd gotten attached to the dog, and the thought of the inn without him almost brought tears to her eyes. Was it time for her to do something to try to make it permanent? And could she really hope that whatever Mike was going to do would save the day?

Andie hauled the flat of petunias out of the trunk of her rental car. She'd been lucky and had snagged some of the pink-and-white-striped variety. Her mother had always used them to edge the garden, but they were rare, and she'd been lucky to find them at the garden store.

The garden was coming along nicely. It should be in pretty good shape by the wedding. It would take longer to fully build out the way her mother had always kept it, though. Maybe if she stayed the rest of the summer... but *was* she going to stay that long? The thought wasn't unappealing. These last few days had made her realize she really didn't have much waiting for her in New York. And Jane needed her here now.

She was treasuring the time with her mother, even with her failed memories. Andie felt like she was getting to know her better on a different level. She'd even brought some of the flowers in on her visit this afternoon and asked for her mother's advice. Addie had lit up. Surprisingly, she hadn't forgotten a thing about planting flowers and proceeded to tell Andie just where to put each color, how to pinch off the leaves for bushier growth, and when to water them.

If she returned to New York, she wouldn't be able to see her mother at all. Even though Addie was in good physical shape, she wasn't going to live forever.

Glancing out at the ocean, she took a deep breath. It was so different from the city here. In New York, when you took a deep breath, you inhaled diesel fumes. In Lobster Bay, it was saltwater and sunshine.

The sounds of hammering made her smile. She was proud of the way the bathhouse was turning out. It had been a lot of fun working with Maxi to design it. They'd picked out fixtures, pored over paint samples, and had even found a few cute decorations. Maxi had a great eye for color and decorating, and the two of them shared a common passion for design. If Andie stayed here in Lobster Bay, she imagined that she and Maxi might even become friends.

She hauled the flat to the garden area, surprised to see a man with a young toddler there. The toddler laughed and pointed at the hummingbird feeder as the tiny brightly colored birds buzzed around it.

She laid the flat down on the ground and paused to watch. Andie never regretted not having children, but the baby tugged at her heartstrings. Grandchildren might have been nice. Still crouched at the child's level, she called out, "Magical, aren't they?"

The child turned to her, smiling, but before he could answer, someone yelled from behind her.

"There's my favorite boy!"

Her heart leaped at the familiar voice. It was Shane, and he was coming toward them. He swooped in and scooped up the child, holding him up in the air. The child kicked and screeched with delight.

He turned to Andie. "Hi, Andie. This is my grandson, Caleb." He settled Caleb on his hip. "Can you say *hi*?"

The little boy smiled and flexed his chubby fingers at her, and Andie couldn't help but smile and wave back.

"Looks like me, don't you think?"

Andie glanced between the two of them, her lips tugging in a smile. "He's much more handsome."

Shane laughed then introduced the man. "This is my son, Greg. And this is Caleb. Greg, Andie Miller. Her family owns Tides."

Andie shook hands with Greg then returned her attention to the baby. Shane tickled him, and he laughed hysterically. It helped ease the tension. Why had she been avoiding Shane? It seemed silly now. Clearly, he wasn't mad or holding a grudge. She'd been making too much of their past. In fact, it looked like he didn't even remember their teen romance or the way she'd broken things off.

One of the reasons she'd avoided Lobster Bay all these years was because she felt guilty about the way she'd ended things with Shane. Now she felt foolish and self-absorbed. It appeared that Shane had moved on from her years ago. He'd been married and now had children and grandchildren.

Now that she didn't feel awkward with Shane and she was making inroads with her relationship with Jane, she had even more reasons to stay and even fewer reasons to return to New York City.

Shane's heart swelled at the joy in Caleb's eyes. Having a grandchild had changed everything for him. He'd never known he could experience such love. Well, maybe once when he'd been young. And Andie had been that love.

But he was older now, and that had all been in the past, water under the bridge. Yet looking at her laughing with that wicked twinkle in her hazel eyes brought it all flooding back. It didn't help that she still looked much like that young girl he'd fallen in love with. She still wore her hair in that sleek ponytail. She'd filled out a bit, but only in the right places. She was no longer the skinny girl he'd once proposed to.

But Andie was an adult now, with her own life in New York City. She probably had a boyfriend. And a lot of responsibility, if her demeanor since she'd been here was any indication. She wasn't carefree like she had been back in high school. But every once in a while, like now, he caught a glimpse of the girl he once knew in high school, and it made his heart beat faster.

Better not get wrapped up in her again, Shane cautioned himself. She'd hurt him once, and she was only staying in town for a short while. Or was she? He'd overheard some snatches of conversation, and Sally had mentioned some things that indicated she might be having second thoughts about that.

Shane didn't dare get his hopes up. Even if Andie *was* staying, he knew he would have to bide his time if he wanted to get to know the mature version of Andie better. At least she had stopped avoiding him now.

CHAPTER 26

Sitting on the back porch of Tides in the moonlight was one of Jane's favorite ways to end the day. It was peaceful with the wide swath of empty beach in front of her and the vastness of the dark night sky, its billions of stars stretching forever over the ocean. The waves crashing on the beach had a relaxing cadence. The glass of wine didn't hurt either.

Andie opened one of the French doors and poked her head out. "There you are. Want some company?"

"Sure. I have crackers and cheese, if you're hungry. Grab a wineglass." Jane held up the bottle.

Andie disappeared back inside then came back out, juggling a wineglass along with an armful of items. Jane filled Andie's wineglass as she settled into the creaky rocker.

Cooper, who was lying next to the railing, kept his eye on the plate of cheese and crackers as if he were willing a morsel of cheese to drop on the floor.

"I wanted to show you some of the paint samples and fixtures that Maxi and I picked out for the bathroom."

The excitement in Andie's voice was contagious, and Jane's spirits lifted as Andie showed her paint cards, pictures of faucets, and flooring samples. Everything was perfect, from the simple lines of the fixtures to the nautical accents.

"And I found these adorable blue-and-white striped hand towels. Of course, we'll have a hand dryer in there, too, but these will look cute rolled up on a shelf like you would see in a spa."

"That will give it a little bit of class." *Hopefully not too many people use them,* Jane thought, mentally adding up the laundry bill.

Andie took a sip of wine and gazed out toward the ocean. "So, it's all coming together, if we can just get the sewer hookup."

"Yeah, if..." Jane let her voice trail off. She'd waited on pins and needles for the sewer department to call with an opening in their schedule, but so far, nothing. She didn't want to voice what might happen if they couldn't. She'd taken out a loan, rooms were booked, and she didn't have enough money to give everything back. Not to mention the poor bride who was counting on them to host her special day.

Andie reached for a cracker. Cooper's ears perked up.

"Don't worry. It will all work out. I have a good feeling." She chewed thoughtfully. "This was a fun project, and I had fun working with Maxi. I never really got to know her or Claire very well because you guys were so much younger than me in high school. It wasn't cool for seniors to hang out with freshmen."

Jane laughed. "Funny how age made such a big difference back then and not so much now."

Andie washed down her cracker with a sip of wine. "Sure is."

They rocked in silence. Jane felt content sitting here with her sister. It didn't escape her that Andie had stayed longer than her usual two or three days. Was she thinking about moving here permanently? Jane wasn't sure how she felt about that, but she had to admit the last few days with Andie had been very pleasant. She wanted to tell her sister that but wasn't sure exactly how.

"Maxi seemed a little distracted. Is she okay?" Andie asked.

Andie had picked up on that too? Maybe it wasn't

just Jane's imagination. Still, she didn't want to voice her worries to Andie. Maxi and James's relationship was her friend's personal business, and Andie was practically a stranger. "I think so. She's a recent empty nester and trying to adjust."

"Oh, I guess that must be hard."

Jane glanced at Andie. She was staring straight at the ocean, but there was a tenseness in her jaw that indicated maybe Andie had some problems of her own. Well, it would all come out in time.

Andie flipped a piece of cheese to Cooper, who caught it expertly in the air. "Will Cooper be staying on here at Tides?"

"I'm not sure. Do you think that's a good idea? I don't want to do anything that could be off-putting to potential guests."

Andie shrugged. "We have guests now that seem to love him. Maybe it would actually attract guests."

"I like having him here." In fact, Jane couldn't imagine *not* having him here. Mike had said he couldn't keep him in Seattle. What would happen to him when Mike went back home?

"What about Mike?" Andie asked.

Jane glanced over to see Andie watching her. "What about him?"

"Is he leaving? Will he take Cooper?"

"I suppose he'll go back to Seattle at some point." The thought made Jane's chest constrict uncomfortably. "He said he didn't have room for Cooper there."

"How do you feel about that?" Andie asked.

"I'd like Cooper to stay here, but technically he belongs to Mike. Actually, to Mike's grandfather. If he stayed here, though, I could bring him to visit at Tall Pines."

Andie piled some cheese on another cracker. "I meant how you felt about Mike leaving."

Jane frowned. "What do you mean? I guess he's become a friend but…"

Andie snorted. "Friend? I wonder if that's what he'd say. Maybe it's time you thought about letting someone in. You know, besides Cooper. It's been a long time since Brad died. You deserve someone to care about you."

"You mean Mike? I'm sure he doesn't feel that way about me. He probably thinks of me as an older sister. I am quite a bit older than him."

"I doubt that. I've seen the way he looks at you, and besides, you yourself said earlier that age doesn't matter so much once you get to be older."

Jane took a gulp of wine. Was it true what her sister said about Mike looking at her? She was eight years older than him, but when they were together, she didn't feel it. She was uncomfortable with the way the conversation was going and decided to turn the tides on her sister. "I saw you happily chatting with Shane. Looks like you didn't need to avoid him after all."

"I wasn't avoiding him. I just didn't go out of my way to talk to him." Andie's tone was indignant.

"Uh-huh." Judging by the way Andie started rocking faster in the chair and avoided eye contact, Jane could tell there was more to that story. She decided to give her a break and instead asked, "How's the garden coming along?"

Andie relaxed, excitement taking over as she talked about the various flowers she had planted and her plans for future plantings. "Of course, I have to be mindful of budget, but I think in time we can make it as pretty as Mom used to have it."

Jane agreed. But it sounded like doing that might take a while, and she had to wonder once more: Was Andie considering staying permanently in Lobster Bay? And did Jane want her to?

Andie could feel the excitement bubble up inside her as she talked about the garden. She'd forgotten how much she'd loved gardening as a kid. Her current lifestyle in

New York City didn't give her much time to think about gardens. Much of her job consisted of being locked away in dusty attics and moldy basements hunting for valuables amid broken-down castoffs. She hadn't realized how much she missed working outdoors.

Not to mention that rambling on about hydrangeas, petunias, and hostas got her sister off the subject of Shane Flannery. Talking to him in the garden earlier had stirred up old feelings that she'd thought had been long buried.

"You must be eager to get back to your job. It sounds like you missed out on an opportunity, from what Chandler Vanbeck said the other day." Jane's look of concern warmed Andie's heart.

"Yeah, but I think taking some time off is doing me good." Andie hadn't missed the job as much as she thought she would. She was keeping herself busy, and the garden work was important. The bathroom project had been invigorating and a good change of pace. These projects would help bring Tides back to profit, and that was important. But once they were done, would Lobster Bay seem like the same boring small town it had been in her youth, or had her priorities changed?

"The ocean has a way of setting one's perspective." Jane turned to her. "I'm glad you're here. Mom has perked up a lot since you came."

"She has?" Andie hadn't considered that her presence would have a healing effect on their mom.

Jane nodded and picked up the wine bottle. "More?"

Andie held out her glass. "I like Tall Pines. It's a nice place. You did a good job finding it. I'm sorry I didn't help more with that." Whew, there! She'd been working out how to convey to her sister that she felt guilty about not being here to help with those decisions. One small little apology didn't make up for all of it, but it was a start.

"It's been a big help having you here to visit with her, especially with this project." Jane gestured toward the bathroom project and the area where the wedding would be held. "I wouldn't be able to manage it if I didn't have you to help out with visiting her."

Andie settled back and sipped her wine. Jane's words soothed her and removed the doubt that her sister didn't want her here. Would it be possible for her to start over in her hometown? What would she do here? Would she get bored? It was definitely a slow pace, but she was getting tired of the cutthroat antiques business. People didn't realize how much competition there was for the good estates, and one had to be on their A game all the time. Andie wasn't getting any younger, and the constant competition had become a bit tedious. She wasn't exactly excited about the idea of going back and working with Doug again either.

Maybe she would never find that big antiques score here in Lobster Bay, but the town did have other benefits. Not the least of which was that she'd be able to visit her mother every day and reconnect with her sister. Her mother's words came to mind.

The city won't give you what you really want. Your roots are here.

She'd been in the city for thirty years and still felt a void. Her mother might be losing her memory, but apparently her advice was still spot-on.

CHAPTER 27

The inn was fully booked for the wedding, but Jane wouldn't allow herself to feel hopeful. She still hadn't received a call from the sewer department. She'd hoped a miracle would happen and someone would cancel or they'd finish up some other jobs faster. Maybe that had just been wishful thinking.

If she didn't hear from them soon, she'd have to tell the bride there would be no wedding unless they had porta potties. They might cancel, and there would go all her bookings. But it wasn't fair to the bride to wait until the last minute. She might be able to book something more suitable if she had enough notice.

If only Andie could work a miracle like she had with the bathroom situation in the first place. Hadn't

Mike said he thought he could help? She hadn't heard from him since.

As if the universe was reading her thoughts, her phone pinged with a text from Mike. He couldn't make it for breakfast.

Don't worry about payment. You've paid me enough and have been taking Cooper. We're even!

Jane's spirits sank. Mike was saying goodbye. He must be getting ready to go back home and didn't want to get her hopes up about their friendship and so was distancing himself. That meant he'd be thinking of what to do with Cooper.

Jane looked down at the dog sleeping at her feet. "Well, Coop, looks like we might have to do something drastic to stay together."

She clipped the leash on Cooper's collar and went out the back to walk on the beach. Mrs. Weatherlee was seated at one of the round tables Jane had put out for people to dine on the back deck. The old woman called out to her as she started down the steps, "The place looks great!"

"Thanks." Jane backtracked and stopped at her table.

Mrs. Weatherlee seemed delighted to see Cooper, feeding him a piece of bacon and petting him excitedly. "It does me good to see the old place getting a face-lift and a new purpose. Your grandparents would be happy."

"You knew my grandparents?" Jane had never even thought to ask her.

"Oh, sure. Everyone in Lobster Bay knew everyone else back in the day. It's much the same now, at least with the families that have been here for generations, isn't it?"

"Yeah, I guess it is." Though the town had grown and she didn't know *everyone* anymore, Jane felt proud to be part of such a community where the people you did know went out of their way to help out.

"Now, don't you worry dear. Everything is going to be fine," Mrs. Weatherlee assured her as Jane headed back down the steps. Jane wished she could be so sure.

She took Cooper for a brisk walk. Even watching the carefree dog bound along after the sticks she threw didn't raise her spirits. She checked her phone for the millionth time. No call or message from the sewer department. After an hour, she headed back to Tides. She was running out of time.

They detoured over to the bathhouse, where Andie was supervising the offloading of toilets. Jane peeked in the building to see Ralph Marchand on his back under the sink, connecting the pipes. A bag of pastries with the Sandcastles logo sat on the vanity.

"Almost done in here," he said. "I've got another job out in Perkins Cove, but once they get the lines hooked up out at the street, call me and I'll come right over to get things squared from this end."

"Will do." Jane was heartened by Ralph's quick turnaround, but it didn't erase her worry over the fact that everything might be for nothing if the sewer department didn't find time in their schedule.

Cooper suddenly raced over toward Tides. Mike was coming around the corner, but not from the beach as he usually did. He was coming from the front. How odd.

Had he driven and parked in the driveway? Her stomach swooped. Why would he drive here? Was he leaving now and had come to take Cooper?

Mike crouched to pet Cooper then looked up at Jane. "I've got good news."

"You do?" She couldn't imagine what it might be.

"Turns out Gramps still has contacts in the town water and sewer department. He called in a favor and got the connection here at Tides fast-tracked."

"He did? What does that mean, actually?"

Mike looked at his watch. "It means that they're going to be here in two hours to hook up the water and sewer to your bathhouse."

Jane didn't know what to say. Was it really going to happen in time?

At Jane's obvious fluster, Mike grabbed her hand and squeezed. "Looks like you're going to get the bathroom finished in time for the wedding."

CHAPTER 28

*A*ndie stood on the back porch, watching Ralph Marchand hook the sewer and water lines to the bathroom. The town had come and hooked them up at the street, and now Ralph was here to hook everything up to the building and test the lines.

There was an air of excitement about the group gathered around the bathhouse as they watched. Several people stood around chatting. Jane looked happy and the most relaxed Andie had seen her. Claire was handing out scones from her bakery. Maxi laughed as she chatted with Sally. Even Cooper wagged his tail faster than usual.

The door opened, and Chandler came out.

He took a deep breath of air and let it out slowly. "There's nothing like the sea air."

"That's for sure," Andie said.

"Looks like you've got a project going on over there."

"Yes, we're putting in a bathroom so we can hold events and weddings here."

"It's looking good. Well, I'm off back to the city today." Chandler glanced at the ocean. "I kind of hate to leave, but duty calls. Are you staying on?"

Good question. "I'm not sure. My world is about antiques, and this town isn't like the big city. There's not a lot of old antiques."

Chandler frowned. "Oh, I wouldn't necessarily say that. These old towns are rife with treasures. Yankee families never throw anything out. You never know what you could find in these attics." Chandler turned around, surveying the area. "And I hear there's a very old house on the cliff that has some interesting history."

"Sadie Thompson's house. She's in the assisted living facility with my mom." Andie had heard several rumors about the house that ranged from it being the headquarters of Blackbeard the pirate to it being a stop on the Underground Railroad. She didn't believe any of them, but it was the oldest house in town and had been in the same family for generations.

A car horn tooted in the driveway. Chandler reached in his pocket and pulled out a card. "I have to run, but I was wondering if you would give this to Maxi. I'm going to be opening an art gallery, and I'd be interested in talking to her if she ever wanted to do a showing."

Andie took the card. It was made of thick paper with embossed lettering. "I think she might like that. I'll make sure she gets it."

Laughter from over at the bathhouse drew her attention. Claire, Jane, and Maxi were clustered around the little shutters with the starfish cutouts. Someone must've told a joke because they were practically doubled over with laughter. It made Andie smile. It was good to see Jane happy, without the constant worry lining her face. She was lucky to have friends like Maxi and Claire to help her.

Andie didn't have any friends she could depend on like that. She'd been too focused on her career, and everyone in her circle was too busy trying to make a name for themselves to have much time to hang out. But things in Lobster Bay were more relaxed, and there was more time for friends.

Maybe it was time for her to make a change. She started toward Jane, Claire, and Maxi with Chandler's card.

253

Maxi stared down at the card in her hand. It was fancy, made with thick ivory paper and black embossed letters. A show in an art gallery? She didn't think so— she was just a hobbyist.

She glanced over toward Tides, but Chandler was gone. "Thanks. But I don't think I'm ready for that." But even as she said the words, a tiny little flutter of excitement sprouted inside her rib cage.

Suddenly there was a seed of hope for her future. Something that didn't depend on James. Something that was just about her.

She longed to confide in Jane and Claire about her suspicions. Normally they told each other everything, but this was such a sensitive subject. James's reputation was at stake, and she couldn't say it out loud until she was one-hundred-percent sure. All she had right now was a card with a woman's number and a sneaking suspicion.

Then there were the kids to think about. They were grown adults, but she still didn't want to talk badly about their father to them. This was a delicate matter and needed to be handled properly. Though she trusted Jane and Claire implicitly, she wasn't ready to say the words out loud. Not yet.

And besides, Jane was so happy now with things going well at Tides, and things were working out nicely for Claire with Rob. She didn't want to bring them down. There would be plenty of time for that later.

"Everything looks so great. I really appreciate all the help you guys have given me," Jane said.

"It was my pleasure," Maxi said.

Claire shrugged. "I didn't really do anything."

Jane laughed. "You don't have to actually *do* anything. Just being there for me to vent with is enough. I couldn't have done it without either of you."

Jane turned to Andie. "And you were the biggest help of all. Honestly, this couldn't have come together without you, either."

Andie's face flushed. She was pleased by the compliment. Maxi noticed a warm look pass between the sisters. Their relationship was thawing.

Andie slipped her arm around Maxi's shoulders. "Hey, I couldn't have done half as good a job without this lady right here. Teamwork!"

"It was a lot of fun, and teamwork is always good, right, Jane?" Maxi added.

But Jane was no longer paying attention. Her gaze was focused halfway down the beach where Mike Henderson was walking toward the inn. Cooper's tail wagged even faster. Cooper looked up at Jane. She nodded, and he trotted off to meet Mike.

"Will you guys excuse me for a minute? I have something I need to tend to." Jane started after Cooper.

Cooper bounded up to Mike, casting one glance back at Jane as if for permission before demanding Mike's attention. Well, that settled it. There was no way she could let Cooper go to a kennel or be adopted by someone else. Cooper needed her as much as she needed him.

"Did they show up?" Mike asked.

Jane looked back at Tides. "Yes. Everything is all set. Thanks for helping out with that." Jane was happy, hopeful, for the first time in a while. There was just one little problem—Mike was leaving, and that meant she was going to have to do something about Cooper.

"I was happy to help," Mike said. "I'm glad things are working out for you."

"There is something I want to talk to you about," Jane said.

Mike's expression turned curious and perhaps a little hopeful. "Oh?"

Cooper returned to her side, and Jane patted his head. "Yes. I'd like to adopt Cooper."

Mike looked a little disappointed. "Oh."

"I know you'll be leaving soon, and you said you don't have room for him in Seattle. He's settled in at Tides, and I could take him to visit your grandfather." It all came out in a rush. Jane was worried that Mike would say no.

"I think that sounds like a great idea, except you're wrong about one thing. I'm not leaving soon."

"You're not?"

"No. Gramps has really improved since I've been here, and I don't want to take that away from him. I can work from anywhere, and besides, this town is growing on me." Mike looked at her out of the corner of his eye. "And some of the people too."

Jane's heart skipped a beat. She suddenly felt very self-conscious.

"There's just one thing, though," Mike continued.

"What's that?"

"Since you have Cooper with you and we both go to Tall Pines, maybe we could go together sometimes." Mike dug at the sand with the toe of his shoe as if he was nervous about her answer.

"Of course we can. That would be great. And you're still welcome for breakfast any time."

Jane looked back at Tides. From her vantage point on the beach, the new bathroom structure blended in perfectly, as if it was meant to be there. Sally and Shane were putting the finishing touches on the archway while Andie was instructing them where to situate it, probably for the best position to train the roses to climb the lattice on the sides.

The inn was going to be full for the wedding, and Jane had everything under control. And her ads and new website must be working because she'd been getting reservations for several weeks out.

She had a new dog, her sister wasn't leaving right away, and now Mike wasn't either. What more could a girl want?

CHAPTER 29

*J*ane balanced the plate of oatmeal-peanut-butter-chocolate-chip cookies in her hand as she stepped out of Andie's rental car at Tall Pines. The cookies were from an old recipe of her grandmother's and a thank-you gift to Mike's grandfather for pushing the sewer hookup through. The hookup had gone off without a hitch, and the bathroom was complete except for few finishing touches. With that work behind them, Jane and Andie had decided they could both use an afternoon off and came to visit Addie together.

"We'll pop in and visit George first. You'll like him, and I know he'll love seeing Cooper." Jane glanced at the dog, who Andie had on a leash, and Cooper wagged his tail enthusiastically, apparently knowing he was going to see George.

"That was nice of him to do that favor. Actually, it was nice of a lot of people in the town. It's refreshing to see how people went out of their way to help us out. You don't get much of that in the city."

Jane smiled. Andie was right—Lobster Bay was special. The more her sister saw that, the more she might want to stay in town. And Jane had decided she really wanted Andie to stay.

The closer they got to George Henderson's room, the harder Cooper strained on the leash. Jane told Andie to unclip it when they were two rooms down, and Cooper rushed in ahead.

"Cooper! Hey, boy." The joy in George's voice was unmistakable.

Jane poked her head in the room, holding up the tray of cookies. "I brought you a little something to say thanks for helping to fast-track that sewer hookup."

"Cookies?" George's attention wavered from the dog to the cookies. "I love cookies."

"It's my grandmother's recipe." Jane turned to Andie. "This is my sister. Andie, George Henderson."

"Andie. Andie Miller. You know, I think I remember you as a little baby. I knew your grandparents." His eyes narrowed. "Did you move away? Can't understand why anyone would do that."

"I'm beginning to wonder that myself," Andie said as she shook his weathered hand.

George offered them a cookie then proceeded to munch on his. "I hear you're going to be taking care of my friend here." George nodded toward Cooper.

"He's been staying with me at Tides, and I've gotten really attached. I just figured that Mike can't have him in the cottage, and who knows how long he'll be staying in town."

George nodded. "I think Cooper will be in good hands with you."

"Me too. And I can bring him to visit you whenever you want after Mike goes back to Seattle."

"I'm not so sure that Mike is going back. I think he might come to see that there is more for him here in Lobster Bay. And I'm not just talking about the ocean. I think he's met some special people here too." George's eyes twinkled as he glanced at Jane before taking another cookie from the plate.

Jane's cheeks heated. "We'd better go visit our mom. We can swing back afterward and get Cooper if you want to spend more time with him."

"That would be great. Thanks for the cookies."

George turned his attention back to the dog, and Andie and Jane left.

"Sounds like Mike might stay. What do you think of that?" Andie said once they were out in the hall.

"He's just a friend, Andie, but it would be great if he stayed. One can never have too many friends." Jane could feel Andie smirking at her the whole way to their mother's room, but at least her sister didn't say anything more. Jane wasn't sure how she felt about Mike. She liked his company, and there was a hint of attraction, but any thoughts of romantic relationships had died when her husband passed years ago. Or had they? Maybe everyone's advice was right and it was time Jane opened up and let someone in. After all, she'd let Andie and Cooper in, and that seem to be working out okay.

Addie's room was cheery and neat as a pin. But she wasn't in it.

"She's in the living room playing cards." A woman that Jane recognized as a volunteer wheeled past them in a wheelchair. "Follow me."

A small crowd was gathered outside the living room. She recognized some of the people as the children of residents. Her heart leapt. Was something wrong?

She hurried toward the crowd. "What's happened?"

A woman with shoulder-length salt-and-pepper hair turned to her. "Shhh. Nothing has happened." She gestured toward the room. "Look at them. They're having so much fun we didn't want to disturb them."

Inside the room, three residents sat on the sofa watching TV. Two other residents were sitting at a table eating a snack, and five, including Addie, were sitting around the card table.

"I've got a five!" One of the residents slapped a card on the table.

"Go fish," another, whose cards kept falling out of his hands, said.

"I'll raise you a goldfish." Addie added a card to her pile.

"I've got old maid!" a woman with a white bun announced.

The woman next to her frowned at her. "Who did you say was an old maid?"

The woman with the bun thought for a second and then replied, "I am!"

They all burst out laughing, each of them putting down cards and randomly picking up others. They weren't really playing a structured game. It was more like they were pushing the cards around the table, but apparently it worked for them.

"Your mom has made lots of friends. She's fitting in

very nicely here," one of the nurses who'd been standing in the back watching said to Jane and Andie.

Jane's heart soared as she watched her mother laughing and interacting with the other residents. She was animated and truly enjoying herself. "That really takes a load of worry off. They look like they are having so much fun."

"I know. Sometimes I think my mom has more fun when I'm not here," the woman with the salt-and-pepper hair said.

"They don't always make a lot of sense, and they have their issues, but it's as if they speak the same language," the nurse said.

As Jane watched her mother, she felt the burden of worry about her mom lifting from her shoulders. In that moment, she knew that no matter what, her mother was going to be okay.

CHAPTER 30

*I*t took a few days for the reality that things might work out after all to settle in for Jane. *Everything is coming together, and Andie is really bringing the garden to life,* Jane thought as she admired the mounds of pink flowers along the edge of the driveway. Cooper sniffed at a bush with long sprigs of purple flowers, disrupting an orange-and-black monarch butterfly.

"The pink flowers are impatiens. Remember Mom used to plant them?" Andie stood beside her, admiring her own handiwork.

"I remember. She'd replace them with mums in the fall." Jane wondered if Andie was planning on doing the same. Would she be around in the fall?

"Impatiens are annuals, so they have to be removed

at the end of summer." Andie stepped back to get a wider view of the edge of the driveway. "Mums would look great all along here and in some big planters near the bathroom."

"Good idea. Now that everything has been approved and I know the wedding is really happening, it might be smart to spruce the bathroom area up with flowers."

"I'm really glad things are working out, and the wedding is kind of exciting," Andie said.

"Yeah, except the more I talk to the bride, the more I wonder if this is going to be as easy as I thought."

"Oh no. Bridezilla?"

"Maybe. She keeps making strange demands. Like special cake frosting and a particular type of candle."

"Maybe she's just nervous. I'm sure everything will be fine," Andie assured her. "Anyone would be nervous with a wedding coming in two weeks. But look on the bright side. We'll have an inn full of guests and get good experience."

"And bookings are up in general." Jane frowned. "I don't love dealing with the people, though. I'm better with the behind-the-scenes stuff."

"True, but I see you've been stepping out of your comfort zone and interacting with them. It's kind of fun talking to them, isn't it? Meeting new folks from different places. They're usually happy, too, because they're on vacation."

"I don't think it's that fun." Jane hesitated then decided to go for it. "If you think it's fun, though, maybe you should stay on. I could use the help."

A look of surprise flashed in Andie's eyes, but at least she appeared to consider Jane's invitation. "I don't know. I have to admit I like the pace here. At work I spent most of my time indoors, and this is nice." Andie waved her hand to indicate the garden and ocean beyond. "I'm not sure there would be enough for me to do here, though."

"Well, you're welcome to stay as long as you'd like. You might be surprised at how much there is to do." Lobster Bay might not be as busy and hectic as Andie was used to, but what's so great about being busy and hectic? Maybe Andie needed to get out of her comfort zone too.

"I might take you up on that." Andie looked at Jane's outfit. "You look dressed up. Where are you off to?"

Jane had taken an hour to pick out the outfit—a short-sleeved top with a bold black-and- white print that hung at hip level and black linen capris. Black, beaded sandals completed the look. She had to admit it was a nice change from her usual T-shirt and jean shorts, and with her thin frame, she looked pretty good. "Oh, just out to eat."

Mike's car pulled into the driveway, and Jane tamped down the butterflies swarming in her stomach.

"Come on, Cooper, you ready?" She tugged Cooper's leash, avoiding looking at Andie. She was sure her sister was smirking behind her back. It was okay, though, because Andie was right. Jane *was* stepping out of her comfort zone, and not just when it came to running Tides.

Mike cracked open a lobster claw and picked out the meat. There was nothing like good old Maine lobster. That was one of the things that Lobster Bay had over Seattle. The other was Jane Miller.

He snuck a glance at her, thinking of how beautiful she looked sitting across from him at the patio restaurant. The setting sun gave her skin a healthy glow. Behind her, colorful fishing boats and dinghies bobbed in the blue waters of Perkins Cove. The soft, warm breeze ruffled her silver hair and brought out the smell of summer flowers. A seagull flying high above the mast of a sailboat cawed, and Cooper, who had been laying at his feet, stirred. He couldn't ask for a more perfect evening.

Jane dipped a piece of tail meat in melted butter. "This is great. I'm glad the restaurant started allowing dogs."

"Me too. And I'm glad I stayed in town." Mike tried to gauge her reaction. She seemed happy to have him staying here, but he reminded himself to take things slow. They'd been walking Cooper together regularly, and when Jane had accepted his invitation to dinner, he felt they were moving in the right direction. She clearly enjoyed his company, and a good friendship was a solid base to a more intimate relationship. As Gramps had told him, there is no need to rush when you know you've found "the one."

"How is your search for a place coming?"

"I have the cottage for another month, but I've been looking at some condos." Mike slipped a piece of lobster to Cooper. "I'm not in a hurry, though. I'd rather wait and get the perfect place. Maybe you could help me."

Jane looked surprised. "Me? I don't know much about real estate."

"I'm looking more for an opinion. I need someone I trust to keep me in check."

Jane smiled and fiddled with the paper straw in her

drink. "And that person is me?" She looked at him from under her lashes, almost flirty.

"I hope so."

Cooper thumped his tail under the table as if he understood the subtext of their conversation.

Jane took a sip of the drink. "Okay, I'll help you out."

"Great."

Their eyes met, and Mike's heart did a little flip at the promise in her gaze.

His phone dinged, breaking the moment. He looked down. Darn, it was Tiffany! With everything going on, he'd forgotten to block her.

Let's get together when you get back to Seattle.

Mike sighed. She simply was not getting the message that their relationship was over. Yet another reason to stay in Lobster Bay. He'd have to call her and explain things clearly. He didn't want her to linger on thinking they were still an item.

"Something important?" Jane asked.

Mike turned his phone off then looked back up at Jane, giving her his full attention. "Important? Nope. Not important at all. Now, what was it that we were talking about?"

****

Life continues in Lobster Bay in Book 3 - *Making Waves*.

Will Tiffany mess things up for Mike and Jane? Will Andie stay in Lobster Bay? Maxie is in for a big surprise:

Making Waves (book 3)

Join my newsletter for sneak peeks of my latest books and release day notifications:

https://lobsterbay1.gr8.com

Follow me on Facebook:

https://www.facebook.com/meredithsummers

ALSO BY MEREDITH SUMMERS

Lobster Bay Series:

Saving Sandcastles (Book 1)

Changing Tides (book 2)

Making Waves (Book 3)

ABOUT THE AUTHOR

Meredith Summers writes cozy mysteries as USA Today Bestselling author Leighann Dobbs and crime fiction as L. A. Dobbs.

She spent her childhood summers in Ogunquit Maine and never forgot the soft soothing feeling of the beach. She hopes to share that feeling with you through her books which are all light, feel-good reads.

Join her newsletter for sneak peeks of the latest books and release day notifications:

https://lobsterbay1.gr8.com

This is a work of fiction.

None of it is real. All names, places, and events are products of the author's imagination. Any resemblance to real names, places, or events are purely coincidental, and should not be construed as being real.

CHANGING TIDES

Copyright © 2020

Meredith Summers

http://www.meredithsummers.com

All Rights Reserved.

❀ Created with Vellum

Made in the USA
Middletown, DE
13 January 2021